OVERGROWN
WITH LOVE

OVERGROWN WITH LOVE

 SCOTT ELY

THE UNIVERSITY OF ARKANSAS PRESS

FAYETTEVILLE

1993

97 96 95 94 93   5 4 3 2 1

Designed by Gail Carter

The paper used in this publication meets the minimum requirements of the American National Standard for Permanence of Paper for Printed Library Materials Z39.48-1984. ♾

Library of Congress Cataloging-in-Publication Data

Ely, Scott.
        Overgrown with love / Scott Ely.
            p.   cm.
        ISBN 1-55728-294-3. — ISBN 1-55728-298-6 (pbk.)
        I. Title.
    PS3555.L94O93   1993
    813'.54—dc20   93-16392
                                                              CIP

To Susan

Acknowledgments

Stories, or versions of them, first appeared in the following:
"Salvation," *The Ohio Journal;*
"The Horse Trainer's Wife," *The Ohio Journal;*
"The Lady of the Lake," *The Southern Review;*
"The Sniper," *The Antioch Review;*
"Night Vision," *Crazyhorse;*
"Holiday," *Yemassee.*

I wish to thank the National Endowment for the Arts and
the Rockefeller Foundation for grants that made the writing of
some of the stories in this book possible.

CONTENTS

THE LADY OF THE LAKE

Even when I was a kid I wondered how those little towns in Alabama and Mississippi got their names, how someone who lived in a house without windowpanes could muster up the nerve to name a town Athens or Florence or Paris, and that too when what they were naming was no more than an empty space, or at the most a single store and a few houses with the hogs wallowing in the street. So when Defoe Michaels said there was a party at Como, a picture of a villa perched on a mountain above a blue lake came into my mind. That spring I'd studied the Italian Renaissance in my art history course at Ole Miss.

"We could go in your car," Defoe said.

He was leaning against the doorway of the Texaco station watching his father pump gas in my car, which I had bought after a summer spent planting pine trees. I'd been stung by hornets, struck at by more than one rattlesnake, and had my skin frescoed by poison ivy. The car was a 1956 Oldsmobile in almost perfect condition, its chrome bumpers spotless, the silver rocket hood ornament reflected in the wax job I'd spent the morning giving it. Because my father had said he was not going to pay for a degree in art history after I dropped out of pharmacy school, I was going in the Marines in October. Once I finished my tour in Vietnam my plan was to take my combat pay and go to Italy. After that I'd return to college on the G.I. Bill and study art history. At the time I had not thought at all about dying.

I never saw Defoe work in that filling station a single time. He was a gambler, not more than ten years older than me. Defoe was a beautiful man, the proportions of his body perfect, as if he had been chiseled out of dark-veined marble by Michelangelo. His face stood out among those lean, patchy red and white hill faces of the townspeople, and some said there was some Indian thrown in and others claimed some Negro too, which I tried not even to think about when I was around him because he was the kind of man who could tell what you were thinking. Maybe that was what made him such a good poker player. When he looked hard at you, the muscles in his face twitched like they were receiving signals.

"Your daddy let you go?" Defoe asked.

Defoe never drove. I might see him come home on a visit driving around the courthouse square with some woman at the wheel of a big car. The women were all pretty, and I never saw him with the same one twice. No one knew why he didn't drive.

"I go where I please," I said, trying to act casual.

He laughed and stepped off the raised curb, crossing the ten or twelve feet to where I was standing. He was wearing a beautiful summer-weight wool suit, which anyone could see had been made by some New York tailor, and a pair of pointed shoes that you probably couldn't even buy in Memphis. The suit clung to his body, like no department store suit ever would, so you could see and almost feel the smooth flex of muscles and bone and skin. Old Mr. Michaels went around to check the oil.

Defoe looked the car over.

"Nice," he said. "But runs a little rough."

"Carburetor needs rebuilding," I said.

"You come get me at six," he said.

I wondered where the woman was who had brought him. I'd seen her standing with him in front of the drugstore, a pretty woman like all the others.

I paid old Mr. Michaels for the gas.

"You been back to the Tallahatchie?" Defoe asked.

And I could see him, standing naked on the rust-stained bridge girder while I waited my turn beside him, my eyes on the long scar which ran from his right nipple to his shoulder blade. He'd come home with that the first time he left town. Then he dived, his compact, dark-skinned body disappearing into the brown water.

I'd been twelve at the time and too scared to follow.

"Plenty of times," I said. "It's easy."

He grinned and said nothing. Mr. Michaels handed me my change. When I got in the car and started it, Defoe bent down and leaned his arm on the paint-chipped window sill, careless of the rich fabric of his jacket.

"Don't you be late," he said.

We drove toward Como, the setting sun fat and swollen over the hills. Defoe was dressed in a white linen suit with a blue tie. When he pulled a silver pocket flask out of his pocket and took a drink, I thought of what my father would say if he knew I was on the road with Defoe Michaels. But that was one reason I had joined the Marines, to keep from becoming like my father. When I told him I'd joined up, he yelled and called me stupid. Mother cried. I told him I wasn't going to lead a comfortable, safe life. I wasn't going to work in a pharmacy like him every day.

Defoe handed me the flask, and I took a drink. I'd already sweated through my yellow button-down shirt and had loosened my striped tie, once knotted in a neat Windsor. These were the kind of clothes I'd learned to wear that first year at Ole Miss. It was one of those real hot days and wasn't going to get much cooler when it turned dark. Defoe looked like he was sitting on a cake of ice, that suit perfectly white and unrumpled, his hair slicked down so the wind didn't toss it around like it was blowing mine. His pink silk shirt had a big D.M. in baroque white stitching over one pocket.

"You up at the university?" Defoe asked.

"Not anymore," I said.

Then I told him about the Marines.

Defoe grinned and took another sip from the flask. That big swollen sun was now directly over the road, looking like when we topped the next hill we were going to drive right into it.

"Going to Vietnam?" he asked.

"I guess," I said.

I took another drink, the whiskey burning as it went down in a way I was trying to learn to like.

"I lost the station," Defoe said.

I looked over at him but didn't say anything.

"It was in Memphis," he said. "Just got outplayed. That's all."

I thought of old Mr. Michaels pumping gas and never saying much. But he'd lent me tools and given me parts on credit to get the first car I bought running. His wife had Defoe when she was almost forty. Now they both were old. I imagined Defoe telling them as they sat around the dinner table and how they had stopped eating in amazement, their jaws moving slowly on the okra or ham, as Defoe explained in his soft voice how in a card game he had destroyed their lives.

"You bet the station?" I asked.

He looked at me, the muscles in his face twitching.

"I bet money I didn't have," he said.

I concentrated on the road.

"We'll find us a couple of women in Como," he said. "Have us a good time."

"That's right," I said.

I was wondering whether the Michaels would go live with relatives. The station was probably the old couple's retirement, and Defoe had gambled it away. He didn't even seem sorry and that made me mad. It was no more to him than if he had pawned his watch to pay a debt.

I looked at him out of the corner of my eye while pretending to be studying a kudzu-filled ravine.

"Don't you judge me," Defoe said.

"It's none of my business," I said.

"That's right."

I turned off the highway and drove a twisting road that finally dropped down to the lake. It wasn't a real lake. The Corps of Engineers had damned up the Tallahatchie River, and now the town of Como had a lake not five miles from the city limits. Below us were the lights around the spillway, the road running right across the top of the huge, earth-filled dam.

"I felt bad after I lost the station," he said. "Nothing has ever made me feel that bad."

Neither one of us said anything for a long time. I was eager to reach Como and get out of the car. Then Defoe spoke again.

"I lost it and went up to my room and got me a blowjob. She wouldn't let me have her car. I could have won it all back with the car."

I thought of the woman in front of the drugstore. She had long dark hair and wore a blue summery dress with white sandals. I thought of her bending over him, Defoe's body stiff with the tension of the loss and then him coming, momentarily free from all of it. While she still had the taste of him in her mouth, he had asked her for the car keys so he could go back to the table. Now I knew why he didn't own a car.

"You could have done it," I said.

And there was a part of me that believed he could. He looked that confident, sitting there next to me in his white suit, his hand around the silver flask, the other arm propped on the car window.

"Well, it don't matter now," he said. "We'll drink some whiskey. Chase some women."

He laughed and I joined him as we drove across the dam, the lights of Como sparkling in the distance.

The dance, held at the National Guard Armory, was part of the town's annual Lake Como Festival. They had a fish fry, a parade, and a beauty contest. I had been the year before and had a good time.

Inside the barnlike building, Defoe and I went our separate ways across the concrete floor. Every now and then we'd meet and share the flask. I noticed he wasn't dancing but standing here and there in the crowd watching the dancers. It was hot in the building, the flashing lights from the bandstand making his white suit look purple.

Then I finally got a chance to dance with the Lady of the Lake, the winner of the beauty contest. She was dressed in white and wore a pasteboard crown decorated with glitter. Her long blond hair, so straight I could imagine her mother ironing it before the dance, swung loose down her back. The strapless evening dress she wore was staying up fine all by itself. She was barefoot, and since it was a slow dance, I was worried about stepping on her feet.

"I've seen you at school," she said.

Penelope was a year ahead of me. She felt light in my arms as we moved across the floor, cigarette smoke hanging in blue clouds above our heads, her face with those high cheekbones looking up at me. I didn't ever want to stop dancing with her. Just as I was telling her about my going in the Marines, someone cut in. I looked up and saw Defoe with a grin on his face.

"Go find you somebody else," he said.

I stood by the wall and watched them dance. They looked good together, both dressed in white. Defoe was smooth, very smooth, and I didn't care for the way he pulled her close to him like they were already lovers. When the music was fast, Defoe stood almost completely still, just moving his hands while she danced around him. Nobody cut in.

Then I found another girl to dance with and kept looking for Penelope but didn't see her again. When the band took a break, I looked for Defoe. I went out to the car, expecting to see him filling up the flask from the bottle under the seat. He was there all right and Penelope was with him. Defoe was kissing her, their mouths glued together, he standing up tall and straight and she kind of clinging to him.

They heard my feet on the gravel. She stooped down and picked up her crown. He took it from her.

"Her daddy's got a cabin out on the lake," Defoe said. "Let's go out there. She'll fix us something to eat."

We all got in the car, she between us in the front seat. He still held her crown. We passed the flask around.

"Aren't you supposed to stay at the dance?" I asked. "You're the Lady of the Lake."

She laughed.

"Not any more," she said. "Defoe's got my crown. This is my first and last contest. I'm not spending my life dieting myself into pageant dresses. I'm not going to be Miss Mississippi."

Defoe tossed the crown out the window.

"Honey, you already are Miss Mississippi," he said.

I wished I'd said it first and thought of Defoe kissing her by the car. That should have been me. He would drift off and maybe never come back to Como. After the Marines I was coming home. She would still be here, teaching school in one of the nearby towns.

"Drive out to the lake," she said. "We'll dance all night in the cabin. I'll fix y'all breakfast."

I was drunk, but the whiskey didn't seem to have affected Defoe at all. She was just as drunk as me.

She had told me to watch for a turn onto a gravel road just before the road that led to the dam. I'd found the turn and was starting to make it when she put her hand on my shoulder.

"I want to go swimming first," she said. "You drive on up to the dam."

"We'll swim at the cabin," Defoe said.

"No, in the spillway," she said.

I knew she didn't mean the real spillway but the emergency spillway, built to deal with a deluge that would overwhelm the spillway and threaten the dam. The spillway was simply a concrete pathway over the western end of the dam which dropped into a channel that led to the river. The channel had filled with rainwater and was a deep clear pool perhaps five hundred yards long.

"I left my swimming trunks at home," Defoe said.

"We won't need 'em," she said.

At the spillway we stood off behind the car while she undressed. Defoe smoked a cigarette as we listened to the rustle of that gown coming off and then the sound of her wading into the water. He didn't seem to be interested, and I tried to act the same. As we stripped down to our underwear, she swam around treading water and yelling at us to hurry up. He folded the white suit neatly and placed the silk shirt and blue tie on top of it.

"You watch her," I said. "She could drown."

"Come on," she shouted.

Then we waded into the water which in the shallows was as warm as the air but turned cool as it got deeper. I had left the car running, and we swam around in the beams from the headlights.

"Let's swim to the dam," she said.

"It's too far for you, honey," Defoe said.

"Someone could get a cramp," I said.

"I might as well have stayed at the dance and become Miss Mississippi," she said.

She started swimming a smooth crawl, and we followed. As soon as we swam out of the lights and the darkness closed in, I got scared. On both sides rose the walls of the channel, made where the engineers had cut through a hill. I began to feel as if we were swimming in the bottom of a well or a cistern, doomed to swim round and round with no way out. She was much faster than either of us. When I turned over on my back to rest and looked up at the stars, I heard her steady kick in the distance. Defoe floated by me.

"She's a banker's daughter," he said.

Then out there in the darkness, wondering whether I was going to make it to the safety of the spillway, I saw it all.

"It won't work," I said. "She'll never do it."

"But she'd marry you, college boy," he said.

He was treading water now, and I did the same.

"I'm a Marine," I said.

"You'll always be a college boy. You'll come home and finish your college and take over your daddy's drugstore. I'll be out there with nothing."

It crossed my mind that Defoe might try to hurt me. But I was a little taller and heavier than he and those days of diving contests off the bridge were long gone.

"Nobody forced you to gamble," I said.

"Everybody gambles," he said. "Her daddy the banker gambles. He just calls it something else."

Penelope was calling to us to catch up.

"You swim on back to the car," he said.

Just then I heard the engine begin to run rough. It gave a couple of coughs and died.

"You go," he said. "Battery'll run down."

He was beginning to gasp for breath. Playing cards is not a good way for a man to stay in shape.

I turned away from him and swam for the spillway, swimming a slow crawl because I had a long way to go. When I reached it, Penelope was sitting on the lip at the bottom, dressed only in a merry widow bra and panties.

"Where is he?" she asked.

There was a faint splashing sound from the channel. I guessed he was floating on his back and resting and told her not to worry. I hoped he'd turn back to the car and leave us alone to talk. I'd tell her about Defoe, how she couldn't depend on him. I'd tell her about all those women. But instead we heard the steady sound of his swimming coming closer and closer until finally he pulled himself up out of the water and lay on the lip breathing hard. When she helped him to his feet, he put his arms around her. I turned my head away and looked at the headlights which I already imagined were growing dimmer.

"What were y'all talking about out there?" she asked.

"Gambling," he said.

I thought of her winning the Miss Mississippi contest. She could do it. She was even more perfect than Defoe. And then the Miss America title in Atlantic City. Soon the accent would be gone. She'd be in Italy long before me.

"I'm going on the road with Defoe," she said.

I wanted to scream, *No, you can't.* Only through a great effort did I keep my mouth shut. Defoe was looking at me; he knew what I was thinking. I could imagine what she thought the road was going to be like—she standing with her hand on his shoulder while he sat at a poker table. But really what was going to happen was that he would take everything from her and not just money. I noticed the headlights were now definitely fading. The battery was not a good one.

"You better go swim back to the car," Defoe said.

"You go," I said.

"We'll draw for it," Defoe said. "Honey, you get a couple of sticks. Long stick wins."

I heard a snap as she broke a stick in half. Then a couple more as she trimmed them to size.

"You draw first," he said.

I could barely see the sticks in her closed fist, a thin one and a fat one. I chose the thin one, the stick slick and waterlogged, bits of it crumbling against my fingers as I pulled it out of her hand. She handed the other to Defoe. We compared sticks, holding them up against the lighter darkness of the sky.

"They're the same," I said.

She started to laugh and then we were all laughing, laughing so hard that we all sat down on the lip, the sound of our voices echoing off the walls of the channel.

"Both of you go," she said, "case somebody gets a cramp."

Defoe had a hard time with the swim, having to stop and float on his back several times. Neither of us did any talking. When we got close to shore, I picked up my stroke and swam on ahead. As I started the engine, I watched him stagger out of the water, his underwear hanging loose about his thighs. It was clear that he was not going to be able to make the swim again.

"We'll let the battery charge a few minutes," I said. "Then we'll swim back."

Defoe was still breathing hard. He got out the flask and took another drink. Then he offered it to me. I refused. My head was clear from the swim, and I wanted to keep it that way.

"You think I'm doing wrong?" Defoe said.

"It's not for me to say," I said.

"My daddy's gonna lose everything. It's my fault. I've got to do something. You know he's gonna take a job at the chicken plant. He'll never last out there. I get to wear a suit and tie doing what I do. It makes me no different from those lawyers at the courthouse. I dress better than them."

I took the flask out of his hand and drank.

"She'll marry me," he said. "I'll treat her good. She don't want to be a beauty queen. She don't want to go back to the university and make a schoolteacher."

"Her daddy won't give you a dime."

"He might."

So no matter what, he couldn't stop being the gambler.

"You take the car," I said.

He took another drink from the flask and gave me a long look as if he were trying to figure out what the catch was.

"I'm leaving in two months," I said. "You can sell it. Stake yourself to a game. You can pay me back with your winnings."

He laughed.

"I'll sit right here and wait for her to swim back," he said.

"Won't be much attraction for her in that," I said.

He knew I was right. Defoe dressed slowly and carefully. I gathered Penelope's gown and my clothes and put them in a pile on the grass.

"You doing this for her?" he asked.

"No, for you," I said. "For your daddy."

Then I realized that was not true at all.

"I better see that money when I come home," I said.

I tried to sound tough, but I knew it was still the voice of a boy. Defoe was not going to be impressed.

"I pay my debts," he said.

I was thankful that he didn't laugh at me.

"But you got to remember. I'm not as good a gambler as you think. I lose more than I win. It's doing it that attracts the women, not the winning."

It occurred to me that maybe when I returned nothing would be changed: Defoe riding into town in a car driven by some pretty woman and his laconic father pumping gas at the station and my father standing behind the counter at the pharmacy.

For a moment I thought he was going to reach out and take my hand, but we just stood there, our arms at our sides. Then he got in the car.

Instead of driving off he hesitated, his face, illuminated by the dashboard lights, turned toward me.

"You watch yourself in them swamps and jungles," he said.

I started to speak but then he was gone, the tailights glowing red in the darkness. I waded into the water and started my swim to the spillway. Penelope and I would swim back and then—if her father's cabin were not too far—we would walk through the early morning darkness to it. And after dancing the night away on its polished heart of pine floor, we'd sit in canvas chairs on the porch, the sweat cooling on our faces, her hand in mine, and watch the sun rise over the lake.

TIGER HUNTING

John Kane often dreamed of tigers. Now, driving out of Mississippi toward Baton Rouge to bring his daughter home, he remembered how he had shot them out of his helicopter in Vietnam. He felt the controls in his hands again. The dead tiger, dangling from a rope tied to a skid, made the ship hard to maneuver as he flew up and over the edge of the lush greenness of the Annamite Cordellera and down to the base camp. He'd sold the skins in Hong Kong.

John's daughter Sassy was coming to stay with him. This morning her voice had appeared on the phone, a casual light tone, but a higher than usual pitch at the beginning of the first sentence, one he recognized as conciliatory, as if she were calling from a party to ask if she could stay late.

"You'll never guess where I am," she had said.

He'd heard voices in the background, a kind of continuous babble, and a woman's husky voice, not his daughter's, said something he couldn't understand.

Sassy was in the state hospital for three days of observation. His ex-wife Star had panicked and on the advice of the emergency room doctor had put Sassy there. It was not like Star to panic. Star's voice had been calm when he called her to explain that Sassy wanted to come to Jackson.

"That's fine," Star had said. "We aren't good friends right now."

She had sounded sad. Sassy's anger had hurt her. So he hadn't complained about her putting Sassy there.

Star, an elementary schoolteacher, had raised their daughter. She and Sassy lived in a house on the edge of Atchafalaya Swamp. Star had built it in the center of ten acres of pines, doing much of the work herself.

Although he saw Sassy at Thanksgiving and Christmas and two weeks every summer, she was Star's child. They were two women living alone on the edge of the swamp. Sassy, like Star, had come to prefer it that way. Now there was a part of Sassy he could no longer reach. When she came to visit, he took vacation time from his job flying helicopters for a Jackson hospital. They still sat up late eating popcorn and watching movies. But it wasn't the same. She no longer laughed at his jokes during a film; instead, she told him firmly to please be quiet.

It was only thirty more miles to Baton Rouge. The air conditioner kept the August heat at bay. Outside the sun shone fiercely down on geometrical rows of planted pines, the corridors between the trees filled with a dangerous-looking jungle of Spanish bayonet, broom sedge, and evergreen laurel.

He wondered what he was going to say to Sassy.

At the hospital he signed papers and talked with the doctor about her depression. The doctor called what she had done a suicidal gesture. John thought of someone waving, another gesture. The young doctor, who was short and built like a tumbler, thought she was going to be all right. John promised the doctor he would see to it that Sassy went to a therapist.

Afterwards he sat with her in the booth in the restaurant she had chosen, called the Tiger's Den. All along one wall were pictures of tigers. The university's mascot was a tiger; the town was full of tiger signs and emblems. He had forgotten about that. The first one he saw had taken him by surprise.

Sassy took four containers of pills out of her purse, lining them up on the table.

"John, look at all these," she said.

He couldn't see inside the containers. He imagined the pills were pastel colored.

"I don't like to take them," she said. "Now I know what an alligator feels like on a cold morning. Just wiggling my finger. That's an effort."

She laughed.

He grinned nervously at her. She had bandages on both wrists, big flesh-colored Band-Aids you wouldn't notice unless you knew she was wearing them.

"You can talk with the psychologist about it," he said.

"I don't want to do that," she said.

He said nothing. He didn't want to argue with her in the restaurant.

"We'll talk about it," he said.

She smiled at him.

He was struck again, as always, by how much she looked like Star, the same blond hair, the same green eyes. It was as if she had inherited nothing from him. She rested her chin on both hands. One of Star's gestures.

"Do you want to see your mother before we leave?" he asked.

"No," she said.

He was glad of that. He preferred to communicate with Star by phone or letter. She was just too difficult in person. She flew into rages. Once she had thrown every pot and dish in the kitchen out of their second floor apartment. White shards of china and aluminum pots lay scattered about on the asphalt.

"I'll see her when I come back," she said.

The plan was for her to spend the rest of the summer with him and then return to the university at Baton Rouge to finish her senior year.

"She won't come to Jackson," he said.

"I know," she said.

She arranged the containers of pills in a straight line by the side of her piece of uneaten strawberry pie.

"You want my pie?" she asked.

"You sure you're not hungry?"

She shoved the piece of pie across the table to him.

He ate while she watched, her hands fiddling with the containers, like she was playing a shell game. He finished the pie.

"Was it good?" she asked.

"Yes."

"I'm leaving these here."

Her fingertip tapped the top of one of the containers.

"Fine," he said.

The thought of her taking that much medication frightened him.

The possibility of talking about why she had done it and why her mother had committed her for observation in of all places a state hospital got left along with the pills on that tabletop. She slept all the way to Jackson, stretched out in the back seat.

In the night he woke not from a dream but to the sound of music. He fumbled for the bedside lamp. Then he rolled out of bed and put on a pair of running shorts.

When he walked into the living room, still groggy from sleep, the music an assault on his ears, he saw Sassy, dressed in purple nylon tights and one of his T-shirts. She was exercising to a tape on the TV. He could tell she had been doing it a long time because she was covered with sweat. She looked at him and smiled but turned her head back to the TV to follow the routine of the smiling figures, two women and a man.

He switched off the TV. Sassy went through a few more steps and stopped.

"I've got to stay in shape," she said.

He looked at her in the tights, her stomach just as flat as Star's. He recalled Star doing sit-ups every morning.

"It's three A.M.," he said.

"I couldn't sleep," she said.

He didn't know what to say. He waited for her to speak, but she said nothing.

"I've got to be ready to fly tomorrow," he said.

"I'm sorry," she said.

"Are you all right?"

Now he had said it, but she didn't react.

She smiled.

"I'm fine," she said. "I'll stay up and read."

He wanted to suggest that she go to sleep too but decided to leave her alone.

Back in bed, he had a difficult time getting to sleep. Sassy knew he was a light sleeper. His awakening had to be no surprise to her. He should have asked the necessary questions.

The whole affair unnerved him. It was the same feeling he had when making a night landing on the hospital roof. He imagined the tiny illuminated pad, framed with blue landing lights, coming up to meet him. The approach was over the tops of big oaks which marked an old residential section of the city. Below, streetlights slipped in and out of the trees. He always feared for himself and those sleeping people. But finally he slept and did not dream.

In the morning he awoke to the smell of bacon.

He got up and showered. By the time he'd dressed, breakfast was ready: grits, scrambled eggs with big chunks of pepper on them, biscuits, and bacon.

"I got scared last night," she said.

"Of what?" he asked.

Now it was all going to come out, he thought.

"A bad dream," she said.

"Tell me about it," he said.

"I can't remember," she said.

"What's the matter?" he asked.

She held up her wrists.

"Oh, you mean these," she said. "I don't know, John. But I'm going to be fine now. Just fine."

"You come wake me up next time you have bad dreams," he said.

He recalled lifting her small child's body out of bed and holding her against him, her sobs gradually subsiding.

"Sure," she said. "No more midnight dancing. Do you like my bacon?"

"It's good."

"Thanks."

She drank her milk, leaving a white moustache on her upper lip.

They went shopping. He had taken leave to be with her. He bought her a sundress and a new pair of heels. She tried on twelve dresses at one store, modeling them for him while he sat in a chair. The salesclerks were amused.

"Your daughter?" a woman asked.

"Yes," he said.

He liked the idea they might think Sassy was a girlfriend. He still looked young. His hair had not greyed, even around the temples.

At home he came into the living room to find her seated crosslegged on the floor, just like Star liked to sit, with his slide collection spread out around her.

"Have you got a projector?" she asked.

She set up the projector and began loading slides into it. He peeled apples for a pie in the kitchen. Every now and then she called him to identify someone on a slide.

"John?" he heard her call.

"Just a minute," he said. "I'm covered with pie dough."

He finished rolling out the crust, noticing he had not heard the click which meant she had advanced the carousel holding the slides. He washed his hands and walked into the living room.

On the screen was the picture of a tiger hanging head down from a pole. The skin was partly removed, the red, flayed flesh looking startlingly naked. Sergeant Amber held a skinning knife in his hand, smiling for the camera. Amber had been very good at both shooting and skinning tigers.

"It's gross, John," she said.

She had said his name as if she didn't think much of it.

"That was a long time ago," he said. "I didn't know any better."

She asked questions. He explained about Hong Kong.

"How much did you make?" she asked.

"Two thousand a skin," he said.

"Star was pregnant with me then," she said.

"Yes," he said.

He was shooting tigers while Sassy was growing inside Star; he was shooting them while she was being born.

"It's so gross," she said. "I mean, how could you do it?"

"At the time I was just thinking about the two thousand dollars," he said.

"They're endangered."

"I know. It was a mistake. I'm sorry for it."

He didn't want to talk about tiger hunting with her. It was something she wouldn't understand.

"Are there any more in here?"

She tapped the box of slides with her finger, using the same gesture she had with the pill containers.

"I don't know."

He felt uncomfortable being interrogated by her. He resented her righteous attitude.

She spent the afternoon going through the slides. If there were other pictures of tigers among them, she made no mention of them.

John woke from a dream of tigers. It was the same old dream. He had throttled back the turbine, the ship coming down in auto rotation. Tigers had learned to run from the high-pitched sound of helicopter turbines. He thought they heard that high frequency sound long before they paid any attention to the rotor wash. Now there was just the gentle whup, whup, whup of the rotors, the green mountainside coming up below them. Asleep on a rocky outcropping was a beautiful tiger, an ideal tiger, his stripes more distinct, his fur thicker than could be possible for a real tiger. Sergeant Amber grinned and leaned out over the skids with the BAR, his favorite weapon. John listened for the slow chug of the automatic rifle. As the sound of the rifle came, he started to bring the turbine back up to power, to that full-throated whine. But nothing happened as he opened the throttle, that reassuring whine not appearing. And the ship was still dropping, the green mountainside coming up to meet them.

He lay in bed covered with sweat. He looked around in the darkness, listening to the gentle hum of the air conditioner. Then he lay his head back down on the pillow and closed his eyes.

But sleep wouldn't come. He got up to see what was on ESPN. One step into the dark hall he tripped, falling onto something soft. The thick nap of a blanket appeared under his hands. It was Sassy, who lay curled up on the carpet, a pillow under her head and a blanket over her.

As he sprawled over her, she woke up and screamed.

"Sassy!" he said. "It's me."

"John?" she asked.

She put her arms around his neck.

"John, I'm so scared," she said. "I don't want to die."

"You're going to be fine," he said.

Why was this happening? he thought. Was it his fault or Star's fault? Had they sent her careening into adulthood so ill prepared that she had had no chance at all?

"I don't know why I did it," she said.

She began to cry. Her face, like a white flower, was turned up toward his.

"Hush, now," he said.

He took her in his arms, held her close.

She calmed down.

"You go make us some coffee," he said.

They sat on the sofa. She had made the coffee so strong he doubted whether he would get back to sleep. It would be light outside soon.

"Tell me why, Sassy," he said.

"I just get so low," she said. "John, I try not to get low but I do."

She sounded like an adult now.

"You're going to be all right," he said.

He wanted to reach out and stroke her hair, so like Star's, but instead he took a drink of coffee.

"No, I'm not," she said.

"You'll be OK," he said.

But even he heard the empty sound of his words.

So they sat together on the sofa in silence until finally she curled up at one end, her bare feet against his legs, and slept. As soon as she was sleeping soundly, he put on a pair of running shoes and went out of the apartment. He ran along the tree-lined street, the humid air thick and wet in his lungs, running into the light of the rising sun as it came shooting down through the big oaks and pines.

Star called. It was Sassy who answered the phone. He listened to her talk excitedly to her mother. She hung up.

"Star wants me to come home," she said.

"What do you want to do?" he asked.

She shook her hair, the fine blond strands flying, and pulled it up off the nape of her neck. Another one of Star's gestures.

"Can you drive me today?" she asked.

He was relieved that Sassy was going back to her mother. He could still see her occasionally. He would go to her graduation in June.

"I'll get a shower," he said. "Then we'll go."

She talked nonstop all the way to Baton Rouge, riding a high now. Star would have to deal with her when she came crashing down. He thought of meeting Star at the familiar filling station on the highway. The station sat in isolation with a soybean field on one side and a grove of pines on the other. It was a scene that always reminded him of an exchange of prisoners.

"We've got a real tiger," she said.

"What?"

"Mike, that's his name."

He realized she was talking about the school mascot. The tiger appeared at home football games, his cage pulled across the field by the cheerleaders while the crowd roared.

"Yes, I know," he said.

"Let's go see him," she said.

"We'll be late for your mother."

"There's time. I know where they keep him."

They had made good time and were early. He didn't want to spend an hour waiting at the filling station. He regarded her suspiciously. Her use of the word *real* disturbed him. He had never told anyone about his dreams of tigers. There was no possible way she could know.

"Are you sure?" he asked.

"In the basement of the animal science building," she said.

He felt uneasy, the same way flying on instruments always made him feel. You had to trust them and not your instincts, or you would fly the ship into the ground.

"OK, but we need to be on time," he said.

Star would wait exactly fifteen minutes and then leave. It was a twenty mile drive to the house.

He drove across the live-oak-covered campus. They had thirty minutes to see the tiger and then return to the filling station.

He parked in front of the building.

Inside he followed her down a set of stairs and along a long windowless corridor, a thick pipe painted blue running along the ceiling. From somewhere far away came the hum of machinery. They turned a corner. Ahead was a door with a single rectangular pane in the center. Wire was embedded in the glass.

Sassy tried the knob. It was locked. She tugged at it and pounded on the door with the flat of her hand. It was a metal door. He could tell by the sound.

"Hey!" Sassy yelled. "Hey!"

Her voice echoed off the walls of the corridor.

"Look," she said, pressing her face to the glass. "His cage is right there. Come and look."

He looked through the glass. Along one side of the corridor was a row of shut doors, on the other a smooth unbroken wall.

"He's right there," she said. "Right behind that wall."

She beat on the door again, so hard he was afraid she was going to injure her hands.

"Sassy," he said.

She turned to him.

"You can stand right by the bars," she said. "Close enough to touch him."

He thought of waiting at the filling station. The floor of the office was begrimed with grease. A girl with enormous breasts, her nipples as big as silver dollars, a gleaming socket wrench in her hand, smiled from a calendar on the wall.

"Let's go," he said.

She hit the door again, a single slap.

"No one is there," he said.

"I wanted you to see him," she said. "John, he's a beautiful tiger."

She threw herself sobbing into his arms. And he, wanting to comfort her, but fearful of something he couldn't name, held her, wondering if indeed there was a tiger pacing back and forth in a cage on the other side of the wall.

They were late. Star's truck wasn't there. He asked at the station and was told she hadn't arrived.

"Maybe she forgot," he said.

"She would have called," Sassy said.

They waited another fifteen minutes. He decided to drive Sassy the rest of the way home.

They drove first on the highway and then on paved secondary roads and then on narrow gravel roads. He kept making turns and hoped he could remember how to get back to the highway. Then off in the distance he saw the feathery-topped cypresses which marked the Atchafalaya.

Because the swamp was so close to the house, only a quarter of a mile away, twice Star and Sassy had had to escape to the highway by boat during floods. That was how he knew what the house looked like: the wide screened porch, the low-pitched roof, the silver wind chimes hanging from the eaves. Sassy had shown him a picture she'd taken from the boat, the brown water lapping at the bottom of the porch. Part of Star's face was in the picture. She was turned toward the house, her mouth set in a determined expression.   •

"Take a left," Sassy said.

The road had forked.

Up ahead he saw Star's green truck. Star was lying halfway under it, one jean-clad leg stretched out on the gravel and the other bent.

"We've been having trouble with the truck," Sassy said.

They stood together by the truck. It was very hot. He waited for Star to slide out from beneath it so they could talk. But she didn't move.

"Sassy, hand me that crescent wrench," Star said.

Sassy got the wrench out of the toolbox which lay open on the gravel. She knelt down and handed Star the wrench. Star probably had grease on her hands, her clothes covered with the powder-fine brown dust. He heard the sharp sound of metal against metal as she worked.

"John, you can start back," Star said. "I've almost got this fixed."

"I'll wait to be sure," he said. "Need any help?"

She laughed.

"Sure," she said. "Come under here."

He slid under the truck. It was much cooler there. Her blond hair was a bright spot in the darkness. He knew he was going to pretend that all those years they had been talking to each other. Sassy was walking about on the gravel, the stones crunching beneath her feet. Star handed him a pair of pliers and showed him what she wanted held.

"I needed another pair of hands," she said.

"I'm going to listen to your radio," Sassy said.

He heard the door of his car open, then close. The engine started. There was the faint throb of music.

Star worked the wrench, moving it quickly. The pliers twisted in his hand.

"Hold it tight," she said.

He squeezed the handles of the pliers, the metal cutting into his hand. She tugged on the wrench.

"Done," she said.

She lay back on the gravel and let out all her breath at once. He put down the pliers.

"You need a new truck," he said.

"Another five years," she said. "I'm going to keep it running another five years."

He wanted to be careful. Even in conversation he didn't want to fall into easy rhythms with her.

"What's wrong with Sassy?" he asked.

"Ask her, not me," she said.

"She wouldn't say."

"I don't think she knows."

He thought of Star building the house and her life with Sassy. He tried to imagine the interior of the house, the kind of pictures Star would have hung on the walls, and the furniture.

"I don't know," Star said. "She doesn't know. That's why I put her in the hospital. I was afraid."

Instead of looking at Star, he looked up at the rusted bottom of the truck. He thought of Sassy dancing before the TV and then sleeping outside the door of his room. He thought of their visit to the tiger's cage. None of it made any sense.

"You did the right thing," he said.

He looked at her. There were lines around her eyes. In twenty years Sassy's face would look like that. But Star was still beautiful. He saw her ending up as one of those old women who pulled their hair back in tight buns and carried themselves with perfect posture.

"Let's see if this sorry truck will run," she said.

Together they slid out from under the truck into the bright afternoon light.

Star got behind the wheel and started the truck. He went to get Sassy's bag out of his trunk. Inside the car he saw her swaying in time to the music. A series of low notes made the car vibrate. With the bag in one hand, he stood by the window and rapped on the glass. She appeared not to hear. Her eyes were closed; her body swayed in time to the music.

He opened the door, and a wave of cold air spilled out over him. The music was so loud it hurt his ears. She turned it off.

"Time to go?" she asked.

"Your mother's waiting," he said.

He stood on the passenger side of the truck and looked across her to Star.

"You should come up to the house," Star said. "Have a beer."

Sassy turned and looked at Star.

"I've got to get back," he said. "I've got to fly tomorrow."

"Another time," Star said.

"I'll do it," he said.

Sassy leaned over and hugged him, her arms around his neck.

"I don't want you flying on my graduation," she said.

"I'll be there," he said.

He closed the door and stepped back as Star turned the truck around on the narrow road. Then they both waved and the truck drove off. Through the rear window he momentarily saw their blond heads and then all was lost in a cloud of brown dust, which slowly began to settle on him and the roadside bushes. A faint taste of sweetness appeared in his mouth.

As he stood for a moment on the gravel, the insects humming madly from the roadside bushes, images of Sassy and Star flooded into his mind. Then one appeared which caused him to suck in his breath sharply. They were sitting together at a rattan breakfast table in the house whose interior he had never seen. They were eating beignets and licking the sugar off their fingers. And at their feet, its tail swishing back and forth between the cane chairs, its fur thick and luxuriant, was the most perfect tiger he had ever seen.

THE BOAR

They drove up to the Pyrenees from the Côte d'Azur in the intolerable August heat, the temperature over a hundred. The road ran straight and flat, the Maritime Alps rising in the distance on their left, while a few yards away a thick growth of roadside shrubs—box and rosemary and thyme—rippled past. Orchards of oranges and lemons were enclosed by cypress hedges against the ravages of the mistral.

Lorraine sat crosslegged in the front seat of the Citroën, holding ice cubes wrapped in a blue bandanna against the side of her neck. She explained to Justin, who was at the wheel, how she was cooling the blood flow through the carotid artery, a trick she'd learned from her tennis friends. Occasionally she offered him the ice. He preferred the cloth pressed against the back of his neck, and when she did that, he threw back his head and groaned with pleasure. Nancy, a big ungainly woman, lay on the back seat with a plastic sack of ice on her stomach. Justin was worried about her soaking the upholstery of the rented car. She'd promised to be careful.

Nancy hadn't been part of their plans. She was an old college friend of Lorraine's. They'd run into her at a party in Nice, and without bothering to ask him, Lorraine had invited her to come spend a couple of weeks with them at the house they'd rented.

His first sight of Nancy was when Lorraine had thrown her arms around the big woman's neck. The women stood under an orange tree hung with paper lanterns. Below in the harbor a celebration was in progress. All the boats had hoisted colored lights into their rigging. Beyond that circus of light was the sea sweeping off toward Africa, the smooth, even darkness broken quietly here and there by a scattering of tiny lights and in one spot spectacularly by a huge yacht lit up like a palace.

When he walked up, they were talking excitedly. He caught the end of a sentence.

". . . a view into Spain," Lorraine was saying.

From that moment Nancy had been constantly with them.

"She's depressed," Lorraine had said when he'd complained.

"She should go to Paris," he said. "She wouldn't be depressed in Paris."

She buttoned the second button on his shirt that he always forgot, and kissed him.

"I want you to be serious," she said. "*You* wouldn't abandon her if she were your friend."

Justin hadn't been able to think of a reply. So the big woman, who spent most of her time complaining, now filled up the back seat of the car, her thick fingers caressing the bag of ice.

After they passed Carcassonne on the autoroute, banners and pennants flying from the battlements of the walled city, they saw ahead the dark blue outline, the massif of the Pyrenees-Orientales, against the sky.

"There's where we'll be," Justin said, turning his head to address himself to Nancy.

After all, he thought, she was going to stay for only a couple of weeks. Then she was planning to go to Grenoble. Lorraine had mentioned that Nancy wanted to visit an old boyfriend there. Nancy was on leave from her job as an assistant curator of an art museum.

Nancy sighed and lifted the ice to her breasts, wrapping her arms around it.

"You're going to love the house we rented," Lorraine said.

Lorraine explained to Nancy that she'd sleep on a cot on the bottom floor, set into the side of a hill. The bedroom was separated from the cellar by a door.

"It's always cool there," Lorraine said.

"Does it have a view?" Nancy asked.

Lorraine sighed.

"It's cool," Lorraine said. "Just think of how cool it's going to be."

Justin knew it would be a long two weeks.

They left the autoroute and drove up into the mountains on a twisting road, finally reaching a plateau of rolling hills, the outline of the massif now a light brownish green instead of blue. It was evening and the combination of altitude and the fading daylight made it much cooler. The pyramidal pines of the littoral, so perfect in their symmetry that they reminded him of artificial Christmas trees, had been replaced by oaks and hemlocks.

"Could we stop someplace," Nancy asked. "The curves make me sick."

Justin pictured her getting sick in the back seat of the car. He drove slower. The road lost altitude and followed a small stream. Cornfields grew on either side.

"I still need to stop," Nancy said.

"I'm looking," Justin said.

"You could've stopped back there," Lorraine said.

Up ahead Justin saw a road turning off toward the stream. Maybe there was a bridge. Trout might be holding in the eddies behind the pilings. Lorraine and Nancy could go for a walk; he'd stand on the bridge and look at the fish.

He made the turn. On the right was corn and on the left a ploughed field. Then in a corner of the bare field, near the line of trees which marked the stream, he saw it, big and black and shaggy. He hit the brakes.

"Look!" he said. "Look!"

Both women swiveled their heads around.

"What?" Lorraine asked.

Her voice was evenly modulated. She sounded bored.

"In the corner of the field," he said.

He'd flung the door open.

"A bird?" Nancy asked.

A gang of crows swooped above the trees.

"No, a boar," he said. "A wild boar."

"Yes, it is!" Lorraine exclaimed.

She was excited now, her voice at a higher pitch. He was pleased.

"It's ugly," Nancy said.

Justin stepped out into the field, his feet sinking into the soft ploughed earth.

"Soooo—eeeee," he yelled. "Sooo—eee."

He remembered his grandfather calling the hogs in Arkansas, the old man's voice echoing off the cypress along the river.

The boar looked up at him. It clicked its white tusks. He yelled again.

"Justin, be careful," Lorraine called behind him.

Justin now was a little afraid. Those white tusks were dangerous. Perhaps fifty yards separated him and the boar; it was a good twenty yards back to the car. He took another step. He imagined the wound in the thigh, the blood of Adonis on the ground.

The boar snorted and trotted away, its tail held high, its scrotum slapping between its legs. Then it vanished into the trees.

He stood on the bridge and looked down at the clear water, which held no trout, while Lorraine and Nancy strolled off along the road. He sensed that Lorraine wanted to be alone with Nancy so they could talk.

A week passed at the house, set high on the edge of a plateau overlooking the red roofs of the town far below. In the town was a casino. On Saturday nights a rock band played in the garden behind the casino beneath red and green and gold lights strung on wires, the throb of the music drifting up to them as they sat on the balcony and looked across at the dark mountains, ridge after ridge rising abruptly up over into Spain.

Lorraine was gone during the day, working on her photographs of Cathar chateaux in the region. Thankfully, she always took Nancy with her. He sat on the balcony and wrote poetry. This was his first sabbatical.

He often thought of the Cathars. They'd been rooted out by the Inquisition, one by one their fortresses taken, the defenders burned at the stake. To the Cathars the visible natural world was a creation of the devil. He could imagine their devil being pleased with his creation of the squat, shaggy-haired boar.

The owner of the house had constructed a small wine cellar in the low-ceilinged room behind Nancy's bedroom. Sometimes Justin thought of the woman as a bottle of wine going bad, slowly turning sour.

"She wants to have a baby," Lorraine told him one night as they lay in bed together.

Now they were almost to the end of the second week.

"She's plenty young enough," he said.

Nancy was a year older than Lorraine, which made her thirty-two.

"She keeps getting pregnant, but has miscarriages," Lorraine said. "She's having an affair with a married man. He wants her to come back to Virginia. He says he'll marry her and have children. But he's said that before."

"She should go to Virginia," he said.

Nancy's present job was in Los Angeles.

"I don't think she should," Lorraine said.

Lorraine began to tell him about Nancy's adventures with the man.

Usually Justin was interested in gossip, in personal details. But he didn't want to know any more about Nancy. He lay and stared up at the skylight, letting Lorraine's words wash over him as a meaningless babble. The night was clear; overhead was a sprinkling of unfamiliar stars.

"Justin?" Lorraine asked.

"Yes," he said.

"What do you think?"

"I don't know. It's up to Nancy."

They lay together in silence in their bed on the top floor. Justin put his hand lightly on Lorraine's breast, the nipple against his palm. She ran her fingertips over his face, like a blind person tracing the shape of a lover. They had to make love quietly. There was no insulation between the floors, just pine boards nailed to the rafters, like a child's playhouse. Even with the second floor between them, Nancy might hear the groans and sighs of lovemaking.

"She's quit her job," Lorraine said.

"A dumb move," he said.

"They didn't appreciate her talent. She's bought some important paintings for them."

"She could teach."

"She doesn't like teaching."

Justin sat up in bed.

"She can go to Grenoble."

"She called yesterday," Lorraine said. "That friend of hers is getting married."

"So she's going to Virginia, to the married man."

"She's so vulnerable now."

"How long?"

"Another week or so. Then she wants to meet a friend in Milan. They'll go on to Rome."

"She needs to go."

"She hasn't been any trouble to *you*. I talk to her every day. You hardly speak to her. How do you think that makes her feel?"

Instead of Nancy he thought of his work. He'd written two very good poems since they arrived. It was true she was gone with Lorraine most of the day. He agreed she could stay a little longer. Lorraine kissed him; they made quiet love.

Justin was writing at his desk when over the corner of the balcony he saw their car, recognizable by its red license plate, come up the last of the series of switchbacks from the village. He hadn't expected them back until after dark.

Lorraine strode onto the balcony, her camera bag over her shoulder. She walked that way, taking quick short steps, when she was irritated. Nancy, she told him, had gone to sleep downstairs. Lorraine was going to have lunch with him and then try to salvage the wasted morning by visiting a nearby chateau.

Over lunch she explained how they'd driven to a chateau perched high at the end of a narrow, knife-like ridge. They'd stopped at the village below and had a drink in a cafe. Then they'd started up the path to the ruined fortress.

"She was fine as long as there were trees," Lorraine said.

Lorraine described how once they left the tree line, Nancy had sat down on the path and refused to go either up or down. Finally Lorraine had been able to coax her back down the path.

"She says she's afraid of barren places," Lorraine said. "All of a sudden she develops this phobia. Whoever heard of such a thing. It probably doesn't even have a name."

"Cenophobia," he said.

"Well, there's a name for everything isn't there," she said. "What matters is that I lost the whole morning."

He was secretly pleased. Lorraine was getting exasperated with Nancy. He wished the house itself were above the tree line. Then this very day she'd be gone.

"She can take the train to Paris," he said.

Lorraine began to twist a strand of her blond hair, a gesture she used when she was trying to solve some difficult problem.

"We can't abandon her," she said. "If she goes to Virginia and that man rejects her, what'll she do?"

He imagined the standard forms of suicide. Curiously, he couldn't pick what he felt was the correct one for Nancy.

"Another week, at the most," he said.

"I'll talk to her," Lorraine said.

Now Nancy stayed in the house during the day while Lorraine visited chateaux. The first day he expected Nancy would putter about, constantly interrupting him. But instead she slept, not getting out of bed even after Lorraine returned.

Nancy finally rose for dinner, which he'd hoped they were going to have without her. They heard her clomping up the stairs. Lorraine rushed to set her place.

At dinner Nancy was talkative, her face fresh and bright from all the sleep. Justin kept thinking of the steps which would take her home: the train from the village to Toulouse, the train to Paris, the flight across the Atlantic.

When Justin and Lorraine went to bed, Nancy sat on the second floor reading. Justin heard her moving about as she made coffee, the water running and the rattle of the pot on the stove. Then there was the creak of the rocking chair on the floor boards, the chair going faster and faster until it was moving at a furious pace.

"She's going to break the chair," Justin whispered.

He imagined the floor boards giving way and Nancy tumbling into the cellar.

"Hush," Lorraine said. "She'll hear you."

Finally he slept, fearing that heavy sound would enter his dreams.

Every day after that was the same. Justin was left alone to work while Nancy slept. She woke for dinner and spent the rest of the night reading in the room below their bed. During the nights that followed, he grew used to the sound of her rocking and was able to sleep, but woke when she stopped. Lorraine slept soundly through it all.

On the fifth night he was awakened from a sound sleep by Nancy going downstairs, off to sleep, he hoped. He closed his eyes and slept for what seemed like only a few seconds when she was back again, the rocking chair creaking. Light was shooting in through the glass doors which opened up onto the balcony. He woke Lorraine.

They spoke in whispers, their lips only inches from each other's ears.

"She's leaving tomorrow," he said. "I'm buying her the tickets myself."

"I think she'll leave soon," Lorraine said. "Didn't you notice her at dinner last night? She was radiant. It'll be better if it's her idea."

Justin wasn't convinced.

"I'll throw her in the trunk of the car if I have to," he said. "Like one of those turkeys."

They'd seen trussed fowl at an open-air market, the feet of one bird tied to those of another with green twine, the animals lying on the cobblestones with baffled expressions on their faces.

"Nancy is leaving, Nancy is leaving," he chanted, an incantation, in her ear.

"Hush," she said. "She'll hear."

"Nancy in Los Angeles," he said. "Nancy in Virginia."

"You are mad," she said.

He reached out and pulled her close to him. She giggled when he kissed her on the neck. A few feet away Nancy probably heard it all, rocking away, her eyes cast moodily upward.

Justin sat on the balcony and looked over into Spain. Now there was snow on the high peaks. On the plateau the roads were all marked with red tipped poles, so drivers could navigate during the snows. But for now the weather was beautifully mild, and the fields, all turned a soft golden color, were in the process of being harvested. Hunters roamed over them, their dogs belled, the sound of their shots harsh punctuations to the softest of landscapes. Monsieur Limoux, their neighbor, had invited him to go hunting, but he'd declined. He hadn't hunted since he was a boy in Arkansas and had no desire to take it up again.

He wrote a line but crossed it out. He hadn't been able to write. Nancy was still there. Despite his endless discussions with Lorraine about her, she was still there. During the last two weeks, he and Lorraine had made love only three times: on a blanket in the forest, in the back seat of the car during a rainstorm, and in the hotel in town. He imagined the staff laughing at them every time the three went into the hotel bar for a drink. Everyone knew the American couple and their friend lived in the house above the village.

The talk between him and Lorraine was full of deadlines. Nancy will leave in a week or Nancy will leave after this or that chateau has been photographed. Yesterday Nancy had made a sudden and it seemed complete recovery from her fear of desolate places and was accompanying Lorraine again, the object of their journey a chateau in a particularly wild and remote location. Tonight he hoped she'd go to bed early and sleep soundly.

Below he watched their car come up the switchbacks. They were a little early but not early enough to make him fear that Nancy had climbed up to a chateau and suffered a relapse.

Nancy had wanted guarantees from Lorraine at breakfast that morning.

"Is this one far out of the trees?" she'd asked.

"They built them in high places, for defense," Lorraine said. "Why do you think they'd build them in the trees?"

Nancy, sounding hurt, said, "I didn't say that. I'm not afraid any more. I want to go where there's just rock. Where nothing grows."

And Lorraine made apologies, too many apologies he thought. At least finally she was growing weary of Nancy. Never had he seen anyone with as much patience as Lorraine.

Lorraine came up to the balcony alone.

"Poor Nancy," she said.

She sat at the table beside him and told him about photographing that particularly barren site.

"Just a few rocks," Lorraine said. "The Inquisition was very thorough there. I thought she'd be driven wild by the place. But she was perfectly happy."

It was on the trip back that they ran into trouble. The hunters had driven a stag out of the forest. One of the men had wounded it.

"It just appeared on the road," Lorraine said. "It staggered and fell to its knees, like it was praying to us. That's what Nancy said it looked like."

At dinner that night their talk was about the barbaric nature of hunting.

In the morning Nancy was up and out with Lorraine again. She seemed completely renewed. Lorraine reported that Nancy had insisted on carrying the heavy equipment—tripods and heavy lenses—up the steep rock trails to the crumbling fortresses. Lorraine admitted Nancy's visit had been a mistake. That admission, for him, was almost as good as Nancy's departure.

"She's going to leave the day after tomorrow, after we visit the caves," Lorraine said. "It was her idea."

They were lying in bed, talking as always in whispers. Justin had made a reservation for the next day to visit the caves, which contained marvelous paintings made by Magdalenian hunters.

Their reservation was for after lunch, which they ate at a cafe in a small village. Nancy had insisted on wearing a white dress and a pair of white sandals with low heels. Lorraine had warned her that the journey back to the chamber containing the paintings was one of close to a thousand meters and the way difficult and slippery. Nancy had laughed and said that even in the sandals she'd be like a mountain goat.

And she proved to be right. Dressed in a jacket against the chill of the cave, Nancy scrambled effortlessly over the rocks and patches of slippery mud. Twice others slipped and fell, but not Nancy.

Finally they reached the room where the paintings had been made, and their guide asked them to turn off the electric lantern each of them carried. They advanced into the room. One by one the guide put the light of his lantern on the paintings: a startled deer, its muscles tensed for flight, ibex, and everywhere bison. Some of the bison ran free, others had their bodies filled with spears. The guide explained various theories as to why the paintings had been made. Then he shined his light on an enormously pregnant bison, which the artist had drawn in headlong flight across the wall of the cave. A spear protruded from her flank, blood trailing down her leg.

Justin heard a gasp from Nancy. Her light came on; she moved away from them. The guide asked her to turn off her lantern. She fell but was up in an instant. Justin heard her sobbing. Lorraine started to go after her; Justin caught her arm. Nancy was a white form fading away into the absolute blackness of the cave.

"Let her go," he said.

Nancy's light illuminated a huge stalagmite. Justin had a momentary image of Nancy standing and weeping for hundreds, for thousands of years, her tears falling to the floor, a grotesque asymmetrical formation arising from them. Then, as the light moved off, he imagined her taking a wrong turn somewhere, wandering off the clearly marked trail into a labyrinth of passages and chambers where she might stay lost for days, maybe forever.

"I'll go find her," Lorraine said.

"No," he said.

"Let go of me."

She tried to pull away from him, but he held her too tightly.

The guide complained. They were interrupting his talk. Justin and Lorraine stepped back away from the group, into the darkness.

"We're responsible for her," Lorraine whispered.

"No," he insisted. "We're not."

But Lorraine prevailed. They left the group, which was now discussing the matter of Nancy in several languages. The guide, exasperated almost to tears, kept appealing to them to pay attention to him.

They found Nancy sitting on a stone bench outside the shop which sold postcards and posters of the cave paintings. She was missing a sandal; her dress had a streak of grey mud on one side. She was smiling.

"I'm fine now," she said.

And that was all either one of them got out of her. She refused to discuss her conduct.

Nancy moved her cot up to the second floor. She said she'd developed a fear of enclosed places and could no longer sleep in a windowless room.

"I liked those exotic phobias better," Justin told Lorraine. "Anyone can suffer from claustrophobia."

Lorraine said nothing. Lately he had sensed a subtle change between him and Lorraine. She'd become more formal. He wondered if it was Nancy's presence or simply that their young marriage was entering its middle age. The last time they were in the village she hadn't held his hand as they walked from shop to shop. They hadn't made love since she and Nancy had come upon the wounded elk. But it could all be due to Lorraine's embarrassment over her friend's conduct.

Justin suggested they go for a walk. They started toward the town.

"We've got to do something," he said. "Look at us. She's driven us out of our own house."

"She's thinking about going to Italy," Lorraine said. "I could go with her, make sure she gets there all right. You know her Italian isn't very good. It's difficult for a single woman traveling alone. Those Italian men are horrible."

"What about your work?" he asked.

Justin felt a sense of panic. He wanted Nancy gone, but he wanted Lorraine with him. He wanted the idyllic life he'd imagined these months would bring.

"I'm ahead of schedule," she said. "You're behind. Think of what you can get done without any distractions."

"You're right," Justin said. "I haven't written a good line in weeks. *We* should go to Italy."

"Don't be silly," Lorraine said.

They were passing Monsieur Limoux's house. He was loading dogs into the back of his truck, a rifle slung over his shoulder.

"Going to kill things," Lorraine said.

Monsieur Limoux backed the truck out and paused to talk. He was going after boar. They were driving boar today in the Foret de Puivert. Then Monsieur Limoux invited Justin to join the hunt the next day.

Justin accepted. Monsieur Limoux grinned and drove off, the dogs yelping and their bells tinkling.

"I thought you'd given up hunting," Lorraine said.

"If I shoot a boar, I think I'll hang it in the cellar for a few days," Justin said. "Monsieur Limoux told me that's the custom around here."

They had seen a boar, gutted but unskinned, hanging on a butcher's meat hook in the village.

"Ugh," Lorraine said.

"You won't say that when Nancy leaves," he said.

"What?"

"She hates hunting even more than you do. She might leave if I join the hunt. Even that might be enough. But just think what she'll do if a boar is hanging down there."

"*I* don't want it hanging there."

"You'll grow to love it there if she leaves."

Then they quit talking and walked in silence for a long time. They both tried to think of other methods to persuade Nancy to leave but could imagine nothing other than ordering her out of the house.

Nancy was sullen after he casually announced his intention to join the hunt. He'd not discussed his plan further with Lorraine and was unsure how she was going to react. They were having dinner on the balcony. Hawk moths, looking like miniature hummingbirds, were making their last rounds of the flowers.

"If Justin shoots a boar, he's going to hang it in the cellar," Lorraine said.

Justin was startled by her bluntness. He hoped this meant she'd come over to his side, that she'd decided against escorting Nancy to Italy.

"I suppose it will stink," Nancy said.

"Oh, no," he said. "It'll be field dressed. The meat needs to cure."

Nancy then proceeded to ask question after question about the hunting and dressing and cooking of game. Justin, who knew nothing about boar hunting, fabricated most of his answers, drawing mainly on boyhood deer-hunting experiences in Arkansas.

They stayed up and talked until it was very late. When they went to bed, Nancy fell immediatedly asleep and snored.

He imagined Nancy leaving in disgust during the night. They would have coffee on the balcony and laugh about her adventures as she traveled alone on Italian trains.

"She'll go after tomorrow," he said.

Neither of them wanted to consider how childish his plan was. It was as if reason no longer applied to their dealings with Nancy.

"I never thought we'd do something like this," Lorraine said.

"You're not doing anything," he said. "It's worth it if she leaves. You don't really believe she intends to go to Italy?"

"She might if I go with her."

Lorraine leaned over and kissed him.

"I'm worried about her, Justin. She's one of my oldest friends."

"I understand, but she's destroying our life."

"Don't be so melodramatic. I want her to leave too. But it's not *that* bad."

He decided not to point out to Lorraine that she'd given tacit approval to his plan.

"When that boar is hanging in the cellar, she'll go," he said.

He didn't tell Lorraine or even admit to himself that he stood little chance of shooting a boar. Monsieur Limoux, a man in his fifties, had been hunting boar all his life and had never shot one. But Justin clung to the idea of hanging the boar in the cellar and watching Nancy pack up and leave.

"I don't think Nancy will care," Lorraine said.

"I do," he said.

"Let's go to sleep," she said. "Just look at us. We're being irrational."

Lorraine went to sleep almost immediately, the gentle sound of her breathing a counterpoint to Nancy's snoring. He, to his surprise, found it difficult to sleep. It was as if he were twelve years old and the next day was the opening of squirrel season.

Justin was out of bed and dressed several hours before sunrise. It was to be a morning hunt, and Monsieur Limoux had explained that the hunters had to be on their stands before first light. To his surprise the women woke and got up too. Nancy made coffee.

"We can meet you after the hunt," Nancy said.

Lorraine had spread Justin's topographic map on the table. Nancy indicated a spot on the edge of the forest.

"What's there?" Lorraine asked.

"It's where we had our first picnic," Nancy said. "Justin can meet us for lunch. We'll pick blackberries again."

They had picnicked in a kidney-shaped meadow on the edge of a cliff, marked by a spot on the map where the contour lines ran close together. The meadow had a view of a valley with a ruined chateau set on a ridge above a village.

"I'll never find it," Justin said.

Nancy handed him his compass and folded up the map.

"It's a small forest," she said. "It'll be easy for a woodsman like you."

Justin found himself suspecting that Lorraine had told Nancy of their conversation. He wanted to speak to Lorraine alone but never got a chance. Both women bustled about making their preparations. Then they were in the car, and there was no chance for a private talk with Lorraine.

Justin, his back against a huge hemlock, heard the baying of the dogs off to the south. He decided he'd had enough of hunting for one day. He let his body go slack from hours of standing motionless. He'd asked for this stand because it was close to the meadow. Monsieur Limoux had assured him it was a good one.

He unfolded the map and calculated that the meadow could be reached if he simply walked over the next ridge. He put the rifle, an ancient military Mauser, over his shoulder, and started down the slope among the big trees. The rifle could easily have been "liberated" from some German during the war. Resistance groups smuggled Allied fliers and Jews out of France over the mountain trails.

It took him only a few mintues to reach the top of the ridge. But instead of the meadow below and the cliff, there was only ridge after evergreen-covered ridge. He checked the map again and found he'd made a mistake; it was the second ridge over. He worked his way down and then up. The ground was dotted with mushrooms. *Rouges,* the neighbors called them. After lunch they'd return to gather them.

At the bottom of the ridge, he followed the curve of it, searching for an easy way up, but it was too steep, the face covered with thorn bushes and saplings growing only a few inches apart. He startled something, a stag he thought, and heard it go bounding off though the underbrush.

He came upon an old logging road and followed it, the track overgrown with vegetation. High over the tops of the hemlocks crows swooped about, cawing as they went. The road wound up the side of the ridge. He heard water running somewhere but never saw the stream. Then he reached the top, and below, the edge of the meadow appeared through the trees. He was hungry.

He worked his way down the steep hillside, gradually more and more of the meadow coming into view. He walked around a huge, house-sized boulder, the edge of the meadow perhaps twenty meters away. On the far side Lorraine was sitting on a blanket. She held a glass of wine in her hand. Nancy was out in the middle of the meadow, picking berries.

Justin went down to them. Lorraine saw him and stood up and waved. Nancy glanced at him and smiled but then went back to her berry picking.

"No luck?" Lorraine asked.

"No," he said. "But there're *rouges* over the ridge."

Lorraine clapped her hands in anticipation.

"Eat and then we'll go pick them," she said.

Justin laid the ancient rifle on the blanket. Lorraine poured him a glass of wine. After he ate some cheese and bread spread with pâté, he laid his head in her lap. She felt warm beneath him. She stroked his head.

"I think she's really going tomorrow," Lorraine said. "Then it'll be just like last summer for us."

Justin watched Nancy move about the berry bushes, a determined look on her face.

"If she doesn't go, maybe we'll both take her to Italy," Justin said. "We could go to Venice. You've been wanting to go there."

"Think how difficult she'd be to travel with," Lorraine said.

"Then let her go by herself," he said.

It seemed to him that Nancy's visit was a nightmare from which they were just now awakening. They decided to leave Nancy to the berries and go pick mushrooms.

They filled a market basket with the mushrooms before they started back. From far away the sound of the horn came floating over the tops of the ridges, mixed with the even fainter baying of the dogs. As they were working their way down the hillside to the meadow, the baying and the sound of the bells grew louder. Then, as the dogs struck something on the ridge above, their baying turned hysterical. The dogs came down the ridge in a mad rush, their voices and bells blending into a mad cacophony of sound, something huge and heavy moving in front of them. He heard the shout of a hunter, answered by another man from the next ridge.

"The boar," Justin said.

"Nancy," Lorraine said.

They both went running down the hillside, the mushrooms spilling out of the basket. Justin tripped and fell sprawling in the leaves. He got up and ran after Lorraine, calling at her to wait.

The sound swung around them toward the east end of the meadow. He caught up with Lorraine, the trees opening into the meadow not ten meters away, their view blocked by a clump of saplings and thorn bushes.

They heard a rifle shot, its flat and elongated sound echoing off the ridges. A hunter yelled, then another. A horn blew. They burst out of the cover of the trees into the meadow. And there, not two meters away from the blanket where she had evidently been sitting when she was surprised by the boar, was Nancy, standing over the still animal with the Mauser in her hands.

The dogs swarmed out of the forest, their bells jingling. They sniffed at the boar and at Nancy's legs. Then the hunters appeared, running out of the forest from all directions. They shouted and laughed, clustering around Nancy, who was laughing too. Someone gave her a wineskin. She raised it to her lips and expertly drank, directing the red stream into her mouth.

"Nancy," Lorraine was saying. "Nancy."

Justin put his arm around Lorraine.

"She's all right," Justin said.

Nancy wiped her mouth across the back of her hand and turned to them. Monsieur Limoux was coming across the meadow, shouting something in his patois that Justin couldn't understand.

"Justin can hang it in the cellar," Nancy said.

Justin looked at Nancy's excited face and imagined her arranging a piece of sculpture in her museum, her big hands strong and sure; he pictured her nursing a child. Tomorrow, and he knew he had no reason to feel such certainty, she would go out of their lives on the train to Toulouse. And he saw Lorraine and himself sitting down on Christmas day to eat the boar she had shot, the meat tasting strong and wild and of the forest.

SALVATION

In December the lake had begun to drop. Someone at the dam had turned a wheel or pressed a button to send water cascading down the spillway and into the Tallahatchie, the river's brown water flowing out of the hills into the Delta where it joined with the Yalobusha to form the Yazoo which meandered across the flat land and into the Mississippi. Randall Sparks liked to imagine the journey of the water to the big river. There was a certainty to it that made him comfortable.

Now it was falling at what he estimated to be about a foot a day. They were lowering the water level in preparation for the spring floods. Every day he came to the edge of the bluff to see if the water had fallen low enough for him to reach the mound. It was a game he was playing. He could've waded across or borrowed a pair of hip boots.

Gradually over the weeks he'd watched the mound rise out of the lake, a dark heap of earth surrounded by grey water and red mudflat. It was the only visible sign left of the people who'd lived in the big creek bottom so long ago. Today the drop had been greater than usual. The base of the mound was finally free of the lake, surrounded by bare mudflat with only a narrow strip of water running in front of it for perhaps a hundred yards.

It began to rain as he started along the trail that led down the face of the bluff. After he passed the high-water line from the previous spring, the trail gradually disappeared. He slid down from shelf to shelf left by the dropping water, bits of sandstone jarred loose by his boots rattling down before him.

He reached the base of the bluff and started across the mudflat, his boots sinking deep into the mud as he advanced. Off to the south was the dam, its top barely clearing the low grey clouds. To the north a cluster of dead trees rose out of the lake, marking the backwaters. He crossed the old highway, the crumbling concrete covered by a thin layer of red sediment. The highway came out of the lake to the north by the big creek and ran south along the side of the bluff before it turned out into the lake again and disappeared. Sometimes as he sat on the bluff and looked down on the highway, he wished a car would appear on the mud-covered road, disappearing with it into the lake.

He crossed the strip of water. It rose to near the top of his boots but no higher, and he managed to get across with dry feet. A flight of wood ducks flew low over his head; he heard the rush of their wings and their squeals. After making several passes over the lake, they dropped down behind the mound with set wings.

As he continued across the mud, he wondered if there was anything left. For the last two weeks people had been coming to it in boats. And he realized that for years past, it had probably been dug during every low water. The day before, a man had moored a red inboard in the shallow water off one side of the mound and spent several hours digging with pick and shovel.

Finally he stood before the mound, which rose well above his head to a height of about twelve feet. It was pocketed with holes dug by artifact hunters. Going around one side of it, he expected to see the ducks get up off the water. But there was nothing on the grey water, only the flash of whitecapping waves. They must have flown across to the far side of the lake while his view was still blocked by the mound.

He began to investigate the mound. He soon discovered that the holes covering it were just the new excavations. There were signs of older and deeper ones. It had been picked clean. He decided he'd return after lunch with a shovel. There was always the possibility the hunters had missed something.

He started back toward the bluff where he and Sharon lived in a cabin. It was built on the plan of a double-pen: one square room was the bedroom and the other the kitchen; a roof had been built over the gap between the pens for shelter against bad weather. Instead of taking the trail up the face of the bluff, he went up the boat-launching road that ran down its south side, the end of the concrete launching ramp now separated from the lake by a wide expanse of mudflat.

"You awake?" he asked as he entered the bedroom.

"What time is it?" she asked.

"Almost noon."

She was lying face down on the water bed. As she began to roll over, the bed quaking, he was reminded of what Peed, their landlord, always said about the bed.

"Sparks, go easy in that bed. Don't you flood my cabin."

Then Peed would begin his high-pitched laugher, not stopping until he was red-faced and gasping for air.

Sparks didn't like the man. Sometimes he wondered if Peed himself had really built the cabin or if the job had been done by one of his long-dead ancestors. If Peed had done the work, he would have had plenty of help, for his numerous relations were firmly entrenched on the land between the bluff and the dam.

Sharon was on her back now, looking at him. Part of the blanket slipped off as she sat up and exposed a breast, the nipple drawn up hard and erect, because the cabin was cold in spite of the portable electric heater set on a table in a corner. Usually he would have been aroused, but now he ignored her, thinking instead about the mound. He saw that she had noticed it, knew there would be no afternoon spent in bed.

"The lake must've dropped two feet today," he said. "I walked out to the mound. This afternoon I'm going to dig in it."

"Why would you want to do that?" she asked.

He was disappointed by her lack of enthusiasm.

"To find arrowheads, pottery, maybe even a skeleton," he said.

"Maybe we can go live there when the electric company turns off the power," she said. "But then you might find buried treasure out there. Is that how you're going to pay the bills?"

"Nobody is forcing you to stay," he said.

She was sitting on the edge of the bed now and slipping into her jeans.

"We've got sixty dollars left and fifty of that we owe to Peed on the first of the month. How are we going to eat?"

"Maybe I'll shoot a deer."

"Oh, great. We're going to live off the land."

Sparks wished she were gone, that he had never consented to let her live with him.

She threw herself face down on the bed and was rocked back and forth by the waves. He walked out of the cabin and stood under the shelter of the breezeway looking down at the lake through the steady rain.

They had met at the airport in Dallas. He was changing planes there on his way home from Fort Lewis to Mississippi after being discharged from the army. He had spent six months in the hospital before the army deemed him fit to leave. What had saved him was that he had quit taking the medication that turned his fellow patients into zombies. And the army wouldn't release you until the doctors said you were well. He'd learned to play the game.

He was glad to be out, to be alive. Yet he didn't feel quite as he expected he would. The medical discharge had been his ticket home, but he still felt uncomfortable, as if he belonged not in uniform but in civilian clothes like the men who had received dishonorable discharges at Fort Lewis. They had stayed together in a group, smoking and talking quietly among themselves.

Sharon had come up to him for no apparent reason and started a conversation. She was returning to school at S.M.U. He explained to her that he was out on a medical discharge. As he said it, he wondered why he'd told her.

"What happened?" she had asked.

"They said I cracked up," he had said.

"Did you?"

She wore her red hair in a long braid down her back and as she talked she tugged at it.

"I don't know," he said. "I didn't want to go back to the bush."

"Then it was an act," she said. "You had a good act and fooled the doctors."

"Yeah, I guess that was what happened."

He told her he was going back to Mississippi.

"I don't think I'll go home right away," he said.

"Won't your parents wonder what happened to you?" she asked.

"Yes, but there's just my father. I'll call him."

"Where will you stay?"

He told her about the cabin on the lake he and his father had rented once for deer hunting.

"You still haven't explained why you aren't going home," she said.

"My father, he won't understand about my discharge. He was a sniper in World War II. Once he killed a German at a thousand yards. He paced it off afterwards."

They had stopped talking then. His plane had arrived. They said goodbye.

He was sitting in his seat waiting for the plane to load when he saw the top of her head, the long braid swinging, as she walked down the aisle. She sat down beside him and announced she was going with him. Then he should have told her but hadn't. The army didn't know either, although they'd tried their best to find out. Now they'd lived together for two months, and still he hadn't told her.

The voices and the visions had started the day after he'd killed his first man. The night before he'd seen him coming along the clay trail that in the moonlight looked like a stream of water flowing between the walls of dark undergrowth. When he raised his rifle, the barrel brushed a bamboo stalk, and at the rattle of it the man stopped. Sparks had seen his features clearly, a small, skinny man even for a slope, wearing a khaki uniform topped by a pith helmet. He shot him, pulling the trigger sharply as he had been taught not to do, the muzzle tracking higher at each shot.

The man didn't make a sound but fell backwards on the trail, holding his head with his hands. For a moment Sparks expected him to be borne away by the flow, like a duck shot on a creek. But he lay on the clay that looked like water and didn't move. Instead of the disgust Sparks thought he would feel, he felt pleasure, a warm feeling, like lying beneath the covers on a cold winter night back home.

On patrol the next day he began to hear the voices. They came out of nowhere, and obviously the other members of the squad didn't hear them, for when he looked at their faces, he saw fear and exhaustion but not the wonder he felt. The voices told him a man would die that day. And a few hours later the radio man lay dead in the grass, while they all hugged the earth, searching for the position of the sniper in the treeline. In the days that followed, one by one they were killed, their fate announced beforehand. After three had died he began to warn them. They only laughed at him.

Then one night he saw the source of it all in the light from a flare, that pale face looking just like the one he had seen in all the paintings but this time with a sad smile on his face. The men, mostly new members of the squad now, didn't notice him standing in a half-crouch staring at one fixed spot. Even if they had looked he knew they wouldn't be permitted to see what was reserved only for him.

"Which one of them should die next?" the figure asked.

"I choose?" he asked.

"Ah, but you have been choosing, all of them."

"You—"

"Man is responsible."

"But you came—"

"It was all lies made up by ignorant people. I am not responsible. No one can be responsible."

As the figure continued to speak, Sparks put his hands over his ears, shutting out the words. Then he felt someone pulling him to the ground; a hand was over his mouth. It was the new sergeant. Richards cursed him in whispers and warned him not to speak out again. The next day the voices began, and before sunset Richards was dead.

Sparks went back into the cabin. Sharon was still lying face down on the bed. He told her he was going up to the store. She said she didn't want to go in the rain. He hoped one day he would come home and she would be gone.

He left the cabin and walked up the hill to the store. It was raining harder now. The path he followed had been transformed into a stream. Parked in front of the store was a red pickup with a CB antenna, a loud-speaker mounted on top of the cab, and a spotlight attached to the driver's side by the door. Dogs filled the back of the truck, three foxhounds with their tails erect and curled and two big spotted coonhounds. Rifles rested in the gun rack.

He had seen the truck before. It belonged to Peed's cousins who lived a mile or so up the road. As he went up the steps, passing beneath the sign, which had PEED'S written in faded black letters, the men came out of the store. They were dressed in hunting clothes: boots, canvas pants, and fluorescent orange vests and hats.

"What'll it be today?" Peed asked as he walked up to the counter. "Cash only."

"I've got money," Sparks said.

"Wasn't saying you didn't," Peed said. "I wondered when you folks would get out of bed. Wish I could sleep that late. Course, I might be inclined that way if I had me a good-looking woman."

Sparks didn't try to stop him. Words always came out of Peed's mouth like that. You just had to wait until he was finished.

"Saw you looking at that Indian mound," Peed continued. "Some folks say you can find skeletons there. Me, I ain't got time to go around digging in the dirt. You find any skeletons?"

"I want some twelve-gauge slugs," he said, trying to ignore Peed's chatter.

"To hunt deer?" Peed asked.

"Yeah."

"You ain't got a hunting license, do you? What happens when the game warden comes along?"

"I won't get caught."

"You got the money, I got the shells."

Sparks reached into his jeans and pulled out the change. Sharon had insisted on keeping the food and rent money herself. He laid the money out on the counter where a white spot had been worn through the green top.

"There's not quite enough for five," Peed said, after he counted the money. "But seeing how you're renting from me I'll let you have an extra one anyway."

Peed opened a box of shells, which were kept on a shelf behind the counter, and took out five of them. They were made of green plastic with the lead tips of the slugs recessed at the ends. Peed laid them out on the counter. Sparks scooped them up and put them in his pocket.

"Billy and Leland just told me they're hiring out at the new chicken plant," Peed said.

Sparks nodded to acknowledge that he had heard and walked out of the store. The rain had let up. Down at the cabin he saw Sharon walk from the bedroom across to the kitchen.

When he went into the kitchen, she was at the stove cooking eggs and bacon.

"This is the last of it," she said. "One of us has got to go to work. Or you could ask your father for some money. He offered to help when he was here you know. If I ask my parents to wire money, they'll use that as an excuse to come out here and cause trouble."

The day he had called to let his father know he was home, the old man had come out to see him. He didn't remember ever having a mother. She had died soon after he was born, and he had lived with a succesion of aunts and cousins until he was old enough to go to school. Then he had moved in with his father.

He realized that as far as his father was concerned it would have been better if he'd been killed in battle. At least his father's friends at the VFW could understand that. He and his father talked about squirrel season, but both carefully avoided speaking of his discharge.

"I'm going hunting," he said.

If he killed a deer, they would have meat for the winter. Peed might even trade groceries for some of it.

"For what, a job?" she asked.

He understood why she'd stayed. When you walked off from what your family expected, it was embarrassing to return.

"Like I told you," he said. "Deer."

He took the shells out of his pocket and showed them to her.

"We can't live on deer meat for the rest of the winter," she said. "When the electricity gets turned off, there won't even be a way to cook it."

He stood there looking at the shells in his hand, feeling the weight of them. She had chosen this life; she had walked up to him in the airport. What was happening to her was not his fault.

"There's a way to get money," he said.

"How?" she asked.

"Peed."

He hoped she'd understand, and he wouldn't have to say more. A year ago, a month ago, he couldn't have imagined he'd be saying something like this to a woman. He'd never said he loved her. That made it different. But it was still hard, and he felt as if something inside him had torn loose, like a piece of metal breaking in an engine so that no matter what you did to it, it wouldn't run right.

"What do you mean?" she asked.

"He likes you," he said.

She laughed.

"Tell that redneck it'll cost him five hundred a night," she said.

"I'm serious," he said. "Just one time and we'll have him. You could threaten to tell his wife."

She turned her back to him and poked at the bacon with a fork.

"Maybe a thousand," she said.

"We have to eat," he said.

"Then go to work, go hunting."

He went across to the bedroom and lay on the bed. After a while she came from the kitchen to tell him the food was ready. They sat at the table and faced each other.

"Just this once," she said. "Just to give one of us time to find a job."

"I was kidding," he said.

"No, you were afraid to ask me."

He decided not to answer her, and they ate breakfast in silence. After he finished eating, he went into the bedroom and took the pump gun out of its leather case. She was in the kitchen washing dishes. His father had given him both the gun and case the Christmas before he was drafted. It was the only thing he had asked his father to bring on his visit.

Unscrewing the top of the magazine, he took out the wooden plug, so that now the gun would hold five shells, four in the magazine and one in the chamber. After chambering one shell, he pushed the remaining shells one by one into the magazine. Then he left without bothering to say good-bye to her. But when he reached the top of the hill in front of the store, he saw that she had come to the kitchen window and was waving at him. He waved back.

Once past the store he moved off the road into the pines. Now a cold wind had come up strong out of the northwest. The rain was still falling as a fine mist. There would be only a few hours to hunt, for with the overcast sky darkness would come quickly. He decided to cross the top of the ridge where pines grew and hunt along the creek that drained into the lake by the north side of the bluff. This would keep him upwind of any deer between him and the lake. Today the deer would be taking refuge from the wind and rain in honeysuckle and cane thickets.

He crossed the top of the ridge and began moving downward, the pines gradually giving way to oaks. The rush of the wind in the tops of the pines was replaced by a clacking sound made by the bare branches of the oaks as they rubbed one against the other.

Soon he reached the creek and began to work his way slowly down it, stopping every few yards and standing very still while he searched the trees and underbrush in front of him. At best he knew he could only hope to see part of an antler, an ear, or a leg. And that might pass unnoticed if the deer remained motionless.

After he covered what he estimated to be about half the distance between his starting point and the lake, the wind began to increase, and the clouds dropped down almost to the tops of the trees. He was standing with his back to a hickory when he heard the sound, at first faint and indistinct, causing him to wonder if he had really heard it at all, but then clearer and moving toward him. It was dogs running a deer, three or four of them at least from the sound of the baying. He hoped Peed's cousins weren't on stands in the creek bottom ahead of him. The dogs had begun in the east but now were circling toward the north. He guessed they would drive the deer across the creek not far from where he was standing. He left the tree and ran ahead at a jog, searching the trees ahead of him for a good place to take up a stand. As he crossed a ridge, he saw that ahead the woods opened up some before closing again in a dense thicket of sapling sweet gums, the trees all bunched together only a few feet apart. He took a stand on the edge of them.

The baying was clear and much louder now, no longer broken by the wind. He stood very still as he tried to pick up the sound of hooves on the wet leaves. But the only sound he heard above the rush of the wind was the steady baying of the dogs. The baying grew in volume as dogs and deer approached the creek. He slid back the forearm of the pump and checked the breech to make sure a shell was in the chamber.

As he squatted on the ground, his eyes fixed in the direction of the baying, he began to hear the sound of them running across the leaves. He wondered if the dogs were running a buck or a doe and if it would make any difference if he got a shot. A doe would make better eating. They reached the creek, but that hardly seemed to slow them down. Only the baying changed in tone for a few seconds while the sound was trapped between the high clay banks. Then deer and dogs were in the sweet gums. It sounded as if someone were beating against the trees with an ax handle, the tops of trees thirty yards away quivering. He knew it was a buck. Now for the first time, he was sure it was a buck that was banging into trees with his antlers as he pushed his way through them. Shouldering the gun, he waited.

When the buck came very close, his rack rattling against the trees, his head bent low to the ground, Sparks was ready. But as the gun kicked against his shoulder, the buck didn't go down. The deer kept going as he fired again, this time the slug cutting almost in half one of the saplings. A clean miss. Somewhere in the time after seeing and shooting, the dogs had passed, three of them, a foxhound and two big coonhounds. Peed's cousins' dogs. Now they were gone, and it was as if they never had been there at all, because their passing, the violence and speed of it, should have altered the landscape in some way. But nothing had changed: the sweet gums still rose out of the earth in close-packed ranks on the ground which sloped away to the creek.

In the thicket he found blood on one of the brown, star-shaped leaves. On an oak leaf was one big drop with an air bubble in its center, the redness of it in violation of the brown hues of the winter landscape. With the dogs at his heels, the buck would not lie down in some thicket to die but run until he dropped.

He recalled the death of a deer in Vietnam. It was a tiny thing, no larger than a foxhound. At dusk they had flushed it out of a bamboo thicket. He was walking with his finger on the trigger of the machine gun as always, lost in thoughts of the vision that had recently appeared to him again, and by reflex swung the barrel of the gun on the movement and cut it in half.

Pushing the past out of his mind so he could concentrate on the buck, he trotted off in the direction of the baying, which was moving fast along the creek toward the lake. But the past returned when he began to wonder if he could have stopped the buck with a machine gun.

After the shooting, the members of the squad had stared silently at him, their scorn not concealed by the camouflage paint on their faces. As they squatted in a circle on the edge of the elephant grass, Martin, the new sergeant, had come up close to him, his face only inches away.

"You little bastard," he said in a whisper. "Six months in country and you do something like that. You'll get us all killed."

"I'm sorry," he said, but forgot to whisper, his voice seeming to boom out through the grass.

The members of the squad visibly winced and crouched lower to the ground. They knew he was the only survivor of several squads, and he had never suffered a scratch. Stories about it were being told throughout the brigade.

"God damn you," Martin whispered fiercely. "You do anything else tonight, and I will personally waste your fucking ass."

Martin had to struggle to keep his voice low.

He surrendered the machine gun to the new man Laird and was given the job of walking point. But this had happened before under other sergeants, and he wasn't concerned. What was different was that Martin never let up on him. In the mornings after night ambushes on which they were all required to stay awake, the sergeant always made the same comment.

"Have a good sleep, Sparks?" he asked. "Get plenty of rest? When we get back to base camp, you're getting a transfer."

He waited for the voices to talk of death, but they had ceased to speak to him. And Martin never attempted to kill him during a fire fight as he expected he would. A few weeks later when they were called back to base camp, Martin put him on a helicopter and sent him to II Corps headquarters. There he was met by a corpsman from the hospital.

He followed the corpsman into a room with a row of empty chairs along one wall. In the center of the room a tall black soldier walked back and forth, followed by a corporal with a .45 on his hip. The black soldier's face was set in a grotesque mask, eyes narrowed to slits and teeth clenched together, as he stalked back and forth across the room. Where the patches indicating his rank had once been sewn, there was now a square hole cut in either sleeve. Back and forth they went across the room, the corporal always one step behind. Sparks had looked down at his sleeve to see if his rank was still there. It was.

At the hospital he told them of the voices but not of his vision. He wasn't prepared for them to believe him, but they did. He had expected they would send him back to the bush. He cooperated. He took the pills, which kept the voices at bay, although at times he could hear them buzzing in his ears like the whine of a mosquito. He liked the way the drug made him feel numb.

He talked to the doctor about his childhood, answered all his questions, and tried to tell him what he sensed the doctor wanted to hear. He got better. Just when he thought they were going to send him back to the brigade, they told him he was being shipped back to the states for more treatment and eventual discharge. He was going to live; he would see no more visions and witness the deaths of no more men.

He realized he was lost in the past, not listening to the dogs anymore. As he pushed the war out of this mind, the sound of baying reached his ears again. It sounded as though the dogs were about to drive the deer out of the woods onto the mudflats. The deer would most likely stay in the cover of the trees, particularly if he had been hit hard. But perhaps he was already dead and didn't know it, unable even to respond to pressure from the dogs, only to run in the original direction in which he had aimed himself until the mass of blood, bone, and muscle that remained failed.

Now he was getting close to the lake; the land was dropping and leveling off. There were bunches of sticks and leaves caught up in the branches of trees ten feet above his head from the last high water. It was growing dark beneath the trees; only a few minutes of light were left. Even if the deer went down, it would be hard finding him in the darkness.

Then willows took the place of the gums, oaks, and hickories. Ahead he saw the open space which was the mudflats, and he burst through the line of scrubby willows into the open, immediately feeling a strong, cold wind in his face and the sting of a colder light rain. It was lighter out on the mudflats, and perhaps two hundred yards away, headed up the lake toward the dam, he saw the buck with the dogs strung out behind him. The dogs no longer bayed but ran in silence. The buck was running strong, giving no hint of faltering.

Following the sets of hoof and paw prints, he jogged out onto the grey mudflat. Off to his left the bluff rose high over the lake. Every now and then he noticed what looked like a dark splotch of blood against the light grey mud. He wondered why the deer had chosen to come out onto the mudflats rather than staying in the safety of the trees.

He came around the side of the bluff and onto the reddish mud, the mound springing into view. The deer had almost reached it; the dogs were starting to lag behind. On the bluff above were the lights of Peed's store and the cabin. Far up the lake was the string of lights marking the spillway of the huge, two-mile-long earthen dam. The deer had reached the mound and disappeared behind it. Then the dogs came up and were lost from sight. When neither deer nor dogs came out from behind the mound, he guessed the deer was finally down.

He walked around the side of the mound, expecting to find the buck stretched out on the mud. But the buck was not there. The dogs were casting about, sniffing at the mud. They turned their heads to him, their ears cocked, as he approached. Then they slunk away and headed back toward the bluff. Although he called to them, they wouldn't return. Even though there were few places near the mound where the buck could hide if he was not yet dead, the dogs would have made the job of finding him much easier.

By the mound he found the buck's tracks, even one place where he had stood and pawed at the mud. But it was hard to tell in the rapidly approaching darkness in which direction the tracks led away from the mound, because the mud had been tracked up by the dogs casting about. He looked out over the water and searched its surface for the head of the swimming deer. But there was nothing. A flight of mallards came up the lake, flying low because of the clouds, on their way back to their roost in the backwaters. After making several circles around the mound and finding nothing, he concluded the wounded deer had taken to the water and drowned. But he realized there was always the chance he'd missed the buck in the dark. He decided to go back to the cabin for a light.

As he walked back toward the bluff in the darkness, he wished he had been home during October before the leaves were off the trees and there was still plenty of cover. Then he could've stalked the buck in the woods along the creek.

And once there had been bear and panther in the creek bottom. The men who had built the mound had hunted them, and his ancestors had hunted them with packs of dogs kept for that purpose. They were all gone long ago. But now there were Russian boar, escaped from a game preserve along the river. They were huge animals, covered with coarse black hair, and very dangerous because of their white curved tusks. Next year he might hunt them, but for now he would have to be satisfied with the buck.

By the time he had crossed the mudflat and climbed the bluff to the cabin the wind was blowing harder, and he guessed that before morning the rain would change to sleet. The light was on in the bedroom.

He pushed open the door, the tiny room filled with light opening up to him. A sudden flash of naked bodies in motion before his eyes and then unbelievably there was Peed rolling off her. He could tell Peed wanted to run, but there was nowhere to go. So he began to jump about on the bed, waving his skinny arms, his cock flapping. She was laughing as she was rolled about on the bed, her arms and legs outstretched to steady herself.

Without thinking, he swung the gun on Peed and fired from the hip. The roar of the gun filled the cabin; Peed's cock and balls disappeared. A small geyser of water shot up from the bed and then subsided. Peed lay moaning, face down in the blood-stained water. The water covered the floor in a rush as Peed and Sharon slowly sank down into the frame of two-by-sixes. Sharon began to scream, a sound he'd never heard her make before.

"I got a deer, a big buck," he said. "We'll have plenty of meat now."

Saying this made him feel calm.

Most of the water had run out of the bed by now, and Peed's head had come to rest against the end of the frame.

"Where's the flashlight?" he asked.

He hadn't been able to find it in its usual place on a table by the bed.

She began a new type of scream, a steady wailing sound.

"I'm going for my deer," he said.

He decided he would go to the store for a light.

She said nothing but scrambled up out of the remains of the bed and stood very still against the wall. Peed hadn't moved or made a sound for some time; Sparks guessed he was dead. This time he began to feel the disgust he'd never experienced before. He felt sick. But when he went out the door and into the cold night air, the feeling disappeared. Up at the store Peed's wife came out on the porch and looked down toward him. The bedroom door opened, and he turned to see Sharon, wearing only a shirt, run across to the kitchen.

"Is Amos down there?" Mrs. Peed asked as he came up onto the porch.

"No," he said. "I need a flashlight."

"What kind?"

"One of the big long ones."

He followed her into the store. She took a big flashlight off a shelf.

"Batteries?"

"Yes."

She put the flashlight and batteries on the conter and computed the sale on an adding machine.

"He gave me credit," Sparks said.

After a moment's hesitation, she pushed the white slip and a pen across the counter. He signed it.

"Amos didn't give you no credit," she said.

"Yes he did," he said. "Down at the cabin."

Her head jerked sharply around in the direction of the cabin.

"You said he weren't down there," she said as he started toward the door.

He said nothing and went out of the store.

By the time he reached the mound, the rain, which the strong steady wind blew against his face, had become mixed with sleet. The more he thought about it, the more certain he was that the buck had not taken to the water. Meeting the dogs with his back to the mound would have been a more likely strategy. He was sure he would be able to locate the buck by circling out from the mound. But only the reddish mud appeared in the beam of the flashlight as he walked. After he began to find his own boot-prints everywhere he looked, he decided to give up. Returning to the mound, he sat with his back to it to keep out of the wind and looked up at the lights on the bluff. A set of headlights appeared by the store and began moving down the boat-launching road toward the lake. For the first time since he'd left the cabin, he thought of what he'd done to Peed. He found it didn't concern him, neither the act nor the punishment that would surely come.

Then up from the creek bottom he heard the dogs begin baying again. He climbed to the top of the mound to see if he could hear better. The wind was blowing even harder now, cutting through his clothes. He began to shiver from the cold; sleet rattled against his canvas hunting coat. Then he saw a figure standing at the base of the mound. The flashlight revealed the pale face, his long hair blown back by the wind. He didn't move, and Sparks wondered if the sleet was freezing on him and glazing his face with ice as it was doing now to the branches of the trees in the woods.

On the bluff the headlights had come down to the boat-launching ramp. They belonged to a pickup or a jeep, because the distance of the lights from the ground made the clearance too high for a car. It stopped at the end of the ramp, and two men got out, silhouetted by the headlights. The baying of the dogs was coming closer. They were still in the woods, but it sounded as though they were going to bring the deer out onto the mudflats again. He heard an electric hum and crackle of static from the ramp as someone prepared to talk over a loudspeaker. A spotlight came on and began to sweep back and forth over the mudflat. But it didn't fall on either him or the figure that still hadn't moved.

"You got his," a voice said. "Now we're gonna get yours. We're gonna cut 'em off real slow."

The lights came off the ramp and down onto the mudflat. But he was not concerned with the approaching truck, because the dogs had just brought the deer out onto the mudflats. They were bringing this new deer over the same path as the buck. The baying grew steadily louder. He hoped that the truck coming slowly across the mudflat, its engine high-pitched in low gear, would not cause the deer to try to swing back up to the north.

But it didn't, and the baying increased in volume. They were coming around the side of the bluff now. When they reached the road, he turned on the flashlight. The eyes sprang up out of the darkness, the deer's red and the dogs' yellow. The deer was coming on very fast now, and holding the flashlight beneath the forearm of the pump, he searched for the head. This time he would bring the deer down with a neck or head shot. The light fell on the deer again, revealing the brown coat, the thin scissoring legs, the red eyes, and the great branching antlers that seemed to spread wider than the mound, their polished tines catching and reflecting the light. He started to shoot but decided not to as the buck came on, the dogs at his heels, his red eyes glowing as big as saucers. The deer scaled the mound easily, covering the ground in great smooth bounds, and he felt himself caught up and moving with him, leaving mound, mudflat, lake behind. He no longer felt cold.

The truck reached the mound, and the two men cautiously approached it, one going around either side. But when they faced each other by the water, sweeping their flashlights back and forth over the mud, they found only the dogs. Happy to see the men again, the dogs ran up to be petted.

"That fool must've taken to the water," one said to the other as he played his light over the whitecapping surface of the lake.

HOLIDAY

Ann Faber and Marshall Portugal were both third-year law students who planned to marry after they graduated. Ann was happy in a sort of idyllic way that had come as a surprise. She'd thought she wanted continual excitement: arguments, love-making in the early morning hours in a cluster of oaks on campus known as the Grove, or waking up in Memphis, their arms about each other in a hotel room overlooking the river. And they'd done all that. But a month ago he'd moved into her apartment, and they'd settled into an everyday love that had the feel of strength and endurance to it. She liked to think of the two of them as a couple on a small sailboat circumnavigating the globe. They'd go on and on and never stop.

But now she was worried about spending the Fourth of July weekend with his family at their summer house outside of Jackson. Ever since she'd started thinking about the weekend she hadn't been able to sleep. She kept waking up at three in the morning.

Marshall's father owned chicken-processing plants, mostly in Mississippi. He'd broken every attempt the workers had made to form a union. He underpaid them and bragged about it. And he was constantly receiving violation notices from OSHA. Trace claimed that none of his plants had been out of business a single day because of what any federal agency or union had done. He'd never said any of this to Ann. The three times they'd met he'd been charming; he'd told stories about playing college football that had made her laugh. She read about Trace's problems in the paper. She didn't think Marshall looked at any of the articles, and she was careful not to bring up the topic.

She and Marshall had talked of joining the Peace Corps or of going out West to work on an Indian reservation after graduation. She thought in the end they'd probably go to work for Legal Services. She hoped they'd both get jobs in south Mississippi so she could be close to her mother who lived in Laurel. Her mother was an administrator in the public schools and lately had been having trouble with her heart.

They finished their classes and drove toward Jackson.

"Have you told your father we're thinking about working for Legal Services?" she asked.

"He knows," Marshall said.

He laughed.

"Daddy's not real happy about it," he said. "He'd rather I run the business. But I'm not cut out for that. Besides, George and Donnie are already working for him. That should satisfy him."

George and Donnie, his two older brothers, spent their free time hunting and fishing. She was thankful Marshall wasn't interested in hunting.

"I wish we were going somewhere else this weekend," she said.

He laughed.

"Daddy likes you," he said. "And Mother too. Just as long as we don't talk politics we'll get along fine."

"We should've gone to Memphis," she said.

They'd received an invitation to spend the weekend at a friend's house. There were going to be fireworks on Mud Island.

"They're expecting us," he said.

She said nothing in reply, and for a time they drove in silence.

"When Daddy was a boy my grandfather bought him a Thompson machine gun," Marshall said. "It was legal as long as you had a permit. Then when John Kennedy got shot the FBI paid granddaddy a visit. They knew where he stood. You know, he refused to accept Kennedy half-dollars at that restaurant he owned."

"I didn't know that," she said. "Why that's horrible."

Marshall disapproved of his father's exploits, but sometimes, like now, she thought he admired the old man's flamboyance.

"Oh, it got in all the papers, but then everyone lost interest. He sold the restaurant. That was the end of it."

"Did he hunt with the machine gun?"

Marshall laughed.

"No, he just went out in the woods and shot it from time to time. Practicing for Vietnam, I guess."

"Jesus," she said. "Does he still have it?"

"I don't know. I guess he does."

The summer house was built in the hills between Jackson and Vicksburg and overlooked a pond Marshall's grandfather had built by damming up a creek at the bottom of a ravine. They sat on the screened porch and had drinks. It was just Trace and his wife Michelle. The brothers were off fishing.

"I was talking with Judson Mill the other day," Trace began.

His father was a tall man like Marshall. Trace was sun-tanned from the golf course and looked fit.

Ann knew what was coming. Judson Mill was the chief justice of the Mississippi Supreme Court. She glanced at Marshall, who took a drink from his glass of whiskey and water and squirmed in his chair. Mill had a reputation for deciding cases in favor of his friends. He was one of the reasons there were no unions at any of Trace's plants.

"Judson told me a man like you'd be high on his list for clerk of the court," Trace said.

"I don't think so," Marshall said.

Ann was relieved. Marshall's voice was even and strong.

"We think we're going to live in Laurel," Ann said.

"That's a lovely town," Michelle said.

"Marshall, I don't want you to say yes or no right now," Trace said. "I want you to take the whole weekend and think about it. Then give me an answer to take back to Judson."

"It seems a shame to graduate near the top of your class and then go work for Legal Services," Michelle said. "I don't see how you'll make enough money to live."

Ann wanted to say something, but she held her tongue. She looked at Marshall and saw he was relieved that she had maintained control of herself.

"I won't change my mind," Marshall said. "Couldn't we talk about something else?"

"He's right," Trace said. "This is a holiday." Then he turned to Ann. "My daddy wouldn't celebrate the Fourth of July. I'll bet you don't know why."

Ann pretended she didn't know and let him explain. The Fourth was the date of the fall of Vicksburg.

"But we've gotten away from all that," Trace said. "Nobody celebrates the Fourth like Mississippians."

"Maybe I'll take Ann to Champion's Hill," Marshall said.

He explained that a famous skirmish had been fought there, part of the battle of Vicksburg. Ann hadn't heard the story before.

"You do that," Trace said.

Michelle suggested that they all walk down to the pond where there was a dock. The end was enclosed in screen.

"It'll be cool down there," Michelle said.

They walked down the hill through the oaks to the pond. Marshall had told Ann that he'd spent his summers at the house when he was a boy. Ann imagined him running through the trees and taking the canoe, now resting bottom up against an oak and covered with leaves, out onto the pond.

At the end of the dock was a stack of five-gallon jugs. Marshall read one of the labels on the opaque white plastic.

"You're poisoning the pond?" he asked his father.

"Full of carp," Trace said. "They dig up the bottom. Wallow around like a bunch of pigs. Ruin the water for the bream and bass."

"Bobby," Marshall said.

Trace and Michelle laughed.

Marshall explained. "Bobby" was the name given to a mythical bass that destroyed their tackle when he and his brothers were children.

"Marshall got pulled right off the dock when he was eight years old," Michelle said.

"There went my pole swimming out across the pond," Marshall said.

"He swam after it," Michelle said.

"I had to go in after him," Trace said. "I was wearing that seersucker suit I liked. Had to go change before I went in to work."

They were on the screened end of the dock now, and Trace filled their glasses.

"Poison and the new fish are free," Trace explained to Ann. "Compliments of the State of Mississippi."

Trace went on to explain how the poison kept the fish from taking oxygen out of the water. It would take a couple of days to completely work. The fish would be edible.

"We'll have us a big fish fry," Trace said.

So they sat at the end of the dock and drank. A kingfisher began flying along the edge of the lake in its jerky style of flight, giving a chattering cry. She thought it strange to spend one's holiday poisoning a pond.

"I'll bet there's at least an eight-pound bass in there," Marshall said.

It came as a surprise to her that he was anticipating what would turn up.

"No way," Trace said. "Five at the most."

Ann looked at the dark water and imagined the fish swimming about in ignorance of the poison that would soon suffocate them. It made her feel sick. She tried to start a conversation with Michelle, but she was working on her fourth or fifth drink and seemed to be in a kind of daze, just saying yes or no to Ann's questions. So Ann resigned herself to listening to the men talk of the size of what might lie hidden in that deep black water.

The brothers returned just after dark. Ann and Marshall had cooked dinner for his parents. Trace recognized the good wine Ann had bought. They both had second helpings of the bouillabaisse. George and Donnie came in with big smiles on their faces. Trace got them a beer.

"We must have fifty pounds of spoonbills in the truck," George said.

"Yeah, but now we gotta clean 'em," Donnie said.

George was taller than Marshall. Donnie was short with big shoulders. They were handsome men like Marshall. Both had been married twice and divorced. The children lived with their mothers.

The brothers went out to clean the fish. Marshall took Ann out to watch, leaving Trace and Michelle to watch the Braves on TV. There were four of the strange looking fish, their long bills looking as if they were made of rubber. Ann thought the fish were huge, the biggest at least four feet long. George lopped off the heads and then Donnie, using a pair of pliers, pulled out the flexible backbone. They cut steaks off the carcass.

"What are they going to do with all that fish?" Ann asked.

She was thinking of the additional fish to be harvested from the pond.

"It's for a church fish fry," Marshall said.

"But there'll be so much," she said.

He laughed.

"It's a big church," he said.

She imagined the brothers filling up freezer after freezer until there was not a fish left to catch in the county.

"Are you all right?" he asked.

"Yes," she said.

"Just calm down. You've been doing great. Don't ruin it now."

Ann said he was right. She would calm down. They'd make the best of the weekend. She threw her arms about Marshall and kissed him.

Everyone stayed up late because the ball game went into extra innings, the Braves losing to the Dodgers in the twelfth. Marshall had gone out to the dock with his brothers. Ann sat alone on the porch with a beer and watched the light from George's cigarette. He was moving his hands about as he talked, the cigarette tip describing circles and arcs in the darkness. Trace had gone off to bed, cursing the bad luck of the Braves.

Michelle wandered out onto the porch in her nightgown.

"I put out towels for you in your bedroom," she said.

"Thanks," Ann said.

"George and Donnie never picked on Marshall," Michelle said. "I always found that strange. Marshall has a kind of dignity that protects him."

Ann liked the sound of that. She wished she'd thought of it.

"It's true," she said. "He does."

"You must think we're an unruly family," Michelle said.

"Oh, no," Ann said.

She laughed nervously. Michelle smiled.

Michelle paused and looked out through the screen toward the men on the dock. "I think you're doing Marshall a disservice dragging him off to Laurel."

"He could be dragging me," Ann said.

Ann was relieved that it was out in the open. She had never learned how to talk around a thing as most Mississippians seemed fond of doing. Their idea of politeness. Her ways of looking at the world had been formed in Ohio, not Mississippi.

"If Marshall hadn't fallen in love with you, he'd be clerking at the supreme court next year," Michelle said.

"Then I should feel guilty because he's in love with me?" Ann said.

She wanted to say, "You want him to be immoral like your husband and his brothers. You want him to be evil."

But she managed not to say these things.

"No, I want you to consider what's best for both of you," Michelle said. "You'll be throwing away your training if you go to Laurel."

"That's our mistake to make," Ann said.

"Well, I just wanted to try," Michelle said. "I don't think Marshall will change his mind. I want to be good friends with you. I want you to bring the grandchildren here to fish and swim in the pond. Just like Marshall's brothers."

Marshall and his brothers were walking up from the dock.

"We'll be going to bed," Ann said.

"Sleep well," Michelle said. "There's no place I sleep better than in this house."

Ann didn't tell Marshall about her conversation with his mother. For the first time since she learned they were going to make the trip, Ann slept soundly. They woke early while everyone was still asleep and went off to visit Champion's Hill. Marshall pointed out the Confederate positions, and explained how they had to withdraw back to Vicksburg. Then on the way back Marshall pulled the car off on a dirt track and they made love, the insects singing in their ears.

"I can't make love to you in that house," she said.

She was sitting on top of him in the front passenger's seat, the only way they could manage in the small car. It was already hot. His chest glistened with sweat.

"Sure you can," he said. "Right in my old bed."

"We'll come out here," she said.

He laughed and said he'd do whatever she wanted.

Back at the house they had a late breakfast. Michelle had gone somewhere in the car. Down at the pond Trace and the brothers were out on the pond in a flat-bottomed boat. They were sowing the milky white poison, a cloud of it spreading slowly through the dark water.

"I think it's horrible," she said.

"It has to be done," he said.

"I suppose," she said. "But I get the feeling they're enjoying it."

He paused for a moment and thought. She'd seen him do the same in class.

"They probably do," he said.

They sat on the porch and drank coffee, watching the men crisscrossing the pond in the boat.

Ann felt suddenly very tired and decided to take a nap. Marshall said he'd go see if the men needed any help.

In the room Ann stretched out on the bed and fell almost immediately asleep. She was awakened by a series of loud sounds. She thought at first it was a dream. As she raised herself further from sleep, she was sure it was the TV. Then, finally completely awake, she thought it was firecrackers, for after all this was the Fourth of July. But as the sound came again, she realized it was gunfire, from down by the pond.

Out on the screened porch she stood with Michelle and watched the men taking turns firing the machine gun. Donnie held it at his hip and fired off a burst across the pond. The firing stopped, and he removed the clip from the gun. Marshall handed him another one.

"What are they doing?" she asked. "What are they shooting at?"

"Nothing," Michelle said. "Just making noise. I suppose it's better than firecrackers. One year Marshall almost lost an eye to a cherry bomb."

Ann went out of the house and walked down to the pond, holding her hands over her ears every time the gun fired, just as the spectators on the dock were doing. George now had the machine gun. He stood with it in his hands, looking out across the pond. He seemed to be waiting for something.

Then she saw the kingfisher take flight on the far side of the pond. It flew in great swoops, giving its chattering cry only once, for George was shooting at it with the gun, a stream of brass cartridges tumbling out and sparkling in the afternoon sunlight. The bird disappeared into the trees. George stopped shooting.

"It's like that damn bird is playing a game with us," he said.

"Ears," Trace yelled.

As they all stuck their fingers in their ears, George opened up with the gun. The bird sailed into the trees and escaped again.

They all laughed.

"Ain't that the damnest thing you ever saw," Donnie said.

"You want to shoot it?" Trace asked Ann.

"Sure, why not," she said. "Only I'm not shooting at that bird."

"Honey, nobody's gonna hit that bird," Trace said.

"Give her the earplugs," Marshall said.

Ann stuffed the foam plugs in her ears and picked up the gun. It was heavier than she'd imagined and smelled of oil.

Marshall told her to start with the muzzle low and guard against the recoil.

She put her weight forward, as Marshall instructed her, aimed the muzzle on the water, and pulled the trigger. The gun went off, bucking hard against her shoulder where tomorrow, she knew, there'd be a bruise. The muzzle climbed, the bullets hitting the water with splats and some ricocheting off into the trees. She shot until the gun was empty.

"That's great," Trace said.

He took the gun from her and pushed another clip into it.

"We're celebrating because this is the birthday of the greatest country on the face of the earth," Trace said. "Ears!"

He pointed the muzzle skyward and ran through the whole clip until the gun was silent and smoking in his hands. A smell of cordite and hot metal hung in the air. They all walked back to the house and had a drink.

"They won't intimidate me," Ann told Marshall when they were alone.

"They're not trying to," Marshall said. "But if they were, they couldn't."

She kissed him. They went to help Michelle with dinner.

Something was wrong, Trace said, as he drank his morning coffee. The fish weren't dying as quickly as the directions on the poison containers said they would. George thought they hadn't used enough poison. He believed the pond was deeper than they'd calculated.

"I've sounded every foot of that pond," Trace said. "I know how damn deep it is."

Trace was a little drunk. Ann watched his sons defer to him. Even Marshall.

"Let's get out there and see what floats up," Trace said. "Ann, I guess you and Michelle can drink coffee and talk."

"I'm going too," Ann said.

"It's gonna be hot," Trace said.

He was smiling in a way Ann didn't like.

"I'm going," she said.

"Ann will be fine," Marshall said.

Ann kissed him.

They went out on the pond, Trace in a boat by himself, the brothers in another. Ann and Marshall took the canoe.

The canoe had a small leak, and they had to bail out the water from time to time. There was a long-handled crab net for gathering up the fish.

Ann looked down at the dark water and saw no sign of dying fish.

"Maybe there're no fish in this pond," she said.

"There's plenty of fish," Marshall said.

Marshall paddled the canoe close to shore while she bailed. Then up out of the black water she saw a large fish rise to the surface. It swam feebly on its side in tight circles. One of its eyes seemed to be staring straight at her.

"Look," she said.

Marshall swung the canoe around so he could see.

"It's a big bass," he said.

She maneuvered the crab net under it and lifted the fish out of the water. Her bruised right shoulder was sore, and she had trouble handling the net. The fish didn't struggle. She watched its gill covers opening and closing as it frantically tried to take oxygen out of the air.

Marshall held it up, his thumb hooked in its lower jaw, and shouted to his father and brothers to look. Then he dropped it in the ice chest.

They drifted over the surface of the pond, the fish floating up in twos and threes. The others were finding them too. Then the brothers yelled. They'd found something big. Donnie was pulling it over the side. Marshall paddled the canoe over to them.

"Bobby," he said.

It was a carp of at least twenty-five pounds. Trace had found one too. Three others came to the surface, and they lined them up on the bank.

"Like pigs," Trace said.

They all returned to the boats but didn't find any more carp. Occasionally a bass or a bream would float to the surface. The brothers argued with Trace over the amount of poison he'd ordered. It grew hot.

Marshall paddled the canoe under the shade of one of the trees. The kingfisher flew by and lit on a snag protruding from the shallow water.

"I've been thinking about that clerk job," Marshall said.

"I thought there was nothing to think about," she said.

She felt hemmed in. She wished they'd gone to Memphis.

"I could do it for a year," he said. "Then we could go work for Legal Services."

"Your father has been talking to you," she said.

From across the pond the brothers yelled that they'd found the biggest carp of all.

"Bobby," one of them yelled.

They both laughed.

"No, he hasn't," Marshall said. "I've just been thinking."

Ann was hot, the shade no real respite from the sun, the thick humid air difficult to breathe. She tried to weigh her words carefully before she spoke, tried not to explode in rage.

"Anyone can make money," she said. "We were planning on doing something else."

"I want to do both," he said. "Well, that's not exactly what I mean. I don't care about money. But that clerk job could open doors for me later."

The kingfisher dove for a fish. It returned to the snag with a minnow in its beak. The bird shook its feathers and, turning the minnow around headfirst, swallowed it.

"Don't you see," she said. "Your father will have you working for him before it's over."

"He doesn't need a lawyer," he said.

"You'll end up running the company. Selling chickens. Abusing your workers."

"George and Donnie know how to do that," Marshall said ruefully.

"They're salesmen. That's all. Just look at them. Your father wants you. Don't you see, you'll end up doing just what he's done. They'll suck you in. You'll end up doing things you'll hate to those workers. It'll destroy you. It'll destroy us. You'll help keep everything in this state the same. That isn't what we said we'd do with our degrees."

Ann found herself out of breath as she tried to think of more arguments. She wished she'd stated her case more eloquently.

Marshall looked out across the lake at his brothers. Donnie stood in the bow of the boat with a crab net in his hands.

"I'm not going to run that business," he said.

"Good," she said. "We'll go to Laurel."

"Just so we can take care of your mother?" he asked.

"No, we can go anywhere you want. We can go into the Peace Corps."

"If I give up this chance, I might not have another one," he said.

"I can't decide for you. But you need to know what's going on with your father."

"You told me."

She sensed that he'd turned sullen, that he was angry with her.

"I know it's hard for you," she said. "I love you."

He leaned forward, his hands on a thwart, the canoe rocking from his movement, and kissed her.

A whoop came from the brothers. Donnie waved at them.

"Hey, yawl got to get after those fish," he shouted.

Off by the dock Marshall's father, who was lifting a fish out of the water, had his back to them. Marshall pushed the canoe out into the deeper water, and they started searching again.

At lunchtime they gave up. No more fish were rising to the surface. Over lunch the men discussed whether there were more fish in the lake. Trace kept insisting that what they had seen was, as he put it, just the tip of the iceberg.

Ann spent the afternoon with Marshall on the screened porch. They played chess and talked no more of plans.

That night Marshall wanted to make love, but she told him she still felt uncomfortable in the house. They decided they'd drive the Natchez Trace back to school the next day and stop someplace for a picnic and afterwards make love on a blanket. She hoped they wouldn't make another visit here until after graduation. She fell asleep with her arms wrapped tightly around him.

In the morning she woke just as the sun was coming up. Marshall was sound asleep. She got up and went into the kitchen to make coffee. The water had just started to boil when Michelle came into the kitchen.

"You're like me," Michelle said. "Up early. Trace and the boys could sleep to noon."

They made the coffee and went out on the screened porch. Ann looked down at the pond and was startled by what she saw. It was as if the water were covered with snow. The sunlight glittered off the white bellies of hundreds of fish.

"I suppose that answers the question about how many fish are in the lake," Michelle said. "What a mess."

"I suppose they'll rot and stink," Ann said.

"Those that they don't pick up and clean right away," Michelle said.

"You can't have Marshall," Ann said.

Michelle laughed.

"Honey, hold on," Michelle said. "I haven't even had my coffee."

"I know what Trace wants," Ann said.

"He'd like to leave his company intact to his grandchildren," Michelle said. "You can't blame him for that. George and Donnie are good boys, but they can't run it. Marshall could."

"Well, he won't."

"Maybe it's better if he doesn't. He's happy with you."

Ann looked closely at Michelle. There was no reason for her to lie.

Marshall came onto the porch with a cup of coffee in his hand.

"Look at that," he said. "I guess Daddy was right about the pond."

Michelle went to wake Trace and the brothers.

"Let's eat breakfast and go," she said.

Marshall was standing only a few inches away from the screen, looking at the pond.

"Who would have thought there'd be that many," he said. "They'll be cleaning fish until midnight."

"I want to get back," she said. "I have a paper due."

He took a sip from his coffee and ran his fingertips over the screen.

"You go on back," he said. "I've only got one class. I can afford to miss it. Donnie or George will drive me back. George said something about paying a call at the Grenada plant. That's close. It wouldn't be much out of his way."

Ann walked over beside him. She put her arm around him. Below them the fish glittered in the sun. The kingfisher, a spot of blue and white, swooped over the lake, its cries echoing off the trees on the hillside.

"I want you to come with me," she said. "They don't need you. Those fish can rot."

"It wouldn't be right to leave them," he said.

She could tell he'd made up his mind. She wondered if Trace had planned it this way but then realized that wasn't likely. The fish had just been one of those fortunate accidents. Trace was lucky.

"You do what you think you should," she said.

It was hard for her to say the words, but she didn't want to drive him further into the arms of his family.

"I love you," she added.

He told her he loved her too. He took her in his arms. Over his shoulder, she saw Trace and the brothers come into the kitchen.

Ann drove on the gravel road that ran up the hill behind the house. The road reached the crest and then ran flat on the ridge, a kudzu-filled ravine on one side and the pond and house on the other. Below she saw the three boats on the pond. They had given up on ice chests and were scooping the fish out and putting them directly into the boats, working frantically before the fish began to swell.

Marshall stood in the canoe, mechanically dipping his net in and out of the pond, clearing a path through the smooth carpet of dead and dying fish. He saw the car and, looking up, waved to her. She tapped the horn. Soon she would have him home. Let Marshall stay two days or even three, gutting and scaling fish. He would come home to her. They would make love; they would play chess; they would talk quietly of their life to come.

Then the pond moved out of her field of vision, the road bordered by trees whose leaves were covered with a fine brown dust, and she felt panic. She couldn't get enough air into her lungs, and she opened her mouth like a runner in the latter stages of a long race. She fought the desire to turn the car around. She imagined Marshall methodically crisscrossing the pond, piling the fish into the canoe, and realized there was nothing she could do or say. Although she tried hard to think of some new argument, she couldn't. So she drove onto the highway, the noonday sun glinting off particles of quartz lodged in the asphalt, and examined her despair into the hot afternoon.

THE SNIPER

I'm the Ole Miss Sniper. But nobody knows it. I'm sitting alone in a bar in Gautier, right on the Pascagoula River. It's real nice in the bar in the morning, the varnished bartop shining in the light shooting through the space under the door. I take a sip from my almost empty can of Dixie beer. Then I begin to squeeze the side of the can and release it, not hard enough to make a permanent dent. The metal makes a rhythmical clicking sound which I think is like a heart. But no, it's like a metronome. That's exactly it, a metronome. I read another page of Walt Whitman, who sure didn't write with a metronome.

I've been fired from the local paper plant. I got fired for reading. I'd keep a book in my briefcase and slip it out when I just couldn't stand it anymore. Henry James, the stories of Italo Calvino, a history of Venice. Whatever I'd picked up that week.

I bought the books at a used bookstore which opened up in an old barbershop downtown. It'll probably be out of business before the summer is over. They kept one barber's chair. Sometimes I sit there and read under a brass lamp. I just wandered in one afternoon, drawn by the novelty of buying a book where Mr. Kennedy cut my hair all those years. Now I go by every day and browse and buy whatever interests me. As long as it's cheap. I love the smell of those old books. Yesterday I picked up the Walt Whitman book. I've been reading it ever since. It's the first time since school that I've read any poetry.

The regulars are used to me and leave me alone. They don't come in until late afternoon. Sometimes they ask questions about what I'm reading, but I'm noncommittal. I kind of mutter at them. As long as you don't make a sound that's actually a word, they lose interest. Or maybe they understand. I don't know. All afternoon they sit there almost motionless, like mud turtles lined up on a log.

Mr. Dedeaux, my boss, said I'd been hired to run the computer center, not to read. And he's right. But who could blame me. The machines were keeping track of all those trees being turned into paper and that paper turned into money. They harvest the trees with a machine that has a set of pincers, like a crawfish. Cuts 'em off at the base with one stroke.

"Axes," I used to say to Mr. Dedeaux. "We need a few good men with axes and crosscut saws."

It was a kind of joke, you see, but he never laughed.

I'm sitting here waiting for my girlfriend Alice to show up. We'll go to a movie and have dinner. Then we're going flounder fishing. Of course, you can't do that until after dark. You wade out in the Gulf with headlamps like the kind miners wear and a spear and a bottle of whiskey. Some folks end up spearing their feet after they've had too much to drink. I like it out there in the Gulf on a summer night, the sea and the sky getting all mixed together in the dark.

"Hunter, let me get you a fresh beer," Suzy says.

Me clicking that beer can is driving Suzy crazy. She's a very short woman who has put coke cases behind the bar to stand on so she can see over it. She likes to say, when she gets drunk, that she missed being a midget by half an inch.

"Sure," I say.

She has black hair, penciled eyebrows, and a large head. Her skin is almost translucent, as if it's been pulled thin by being stretched too tightly over her skull. If she had lived in the nineteenth century, she'd have been a phrenologist's delight.

She steps up on a coke case and slides the beer in front of me. I thank her.

I've got a limit. I'm not worried about becoming a drunk. I'm not worried about the fact that my unemployment runs out on Monday. There's a whole weekend before that happens.

Alice, who delivers packages for UPS, is getting off early. I wish I were in the shape that woman is in. She sprints up alleys and dashes up stairs to bring those parcels to the customers. It's hard to do that in Mississippi. People expect you to pause and talk. Pretty soon they'll make a supervisor out of her.

Before I know it the morning is over. I close my book, using a matchbook cover for a bookmark. It's amazing how quick you can learn to make time pass, especially if you have a book to help you.

But now I'm impatient. Alice is late and I'm hungry. The bar fills up. People have walked over from the newspaper office across the street. A cop is sitting next to me in what should be Alice's seat.

Alice comes in. She's changed out of the brown men's pants and those thick-soled shoes into a sundress and white sandals. It's one of those cotton dresses with a narrow high waist that makes her look good. I think she looks like a flower. I order us both shrimp burgers and beer. She apologizes for being late. Then she asks Suzy for a glass. Alice hates to drink beer out of a can. I eat fast and drink the rest of my beer while she finishes. She wipes hot sauce off her hands with a napkin and looks at me like she doesn't think much of what she sees.

"Hunter, I don't want to sit in here all afternoon and drink," she says.

"It's too hot to leave," I say.

At the door the single bar of light quivers, as if the world outside is on fire.

She laughs and pokes me in the ribs.

"We could go to a movie," she says.

"I've seen 'em all," I say. "Some twice."

The cop on the other side of me is working on his second shrimp burger. Then it strikes me that the statute of limitations is long past. There's not a thing anyone can do. I think of the fate of C. J. Whitman, the Texas Tower Sniper. One day he climbed up that tower and killed twelve people. Wounded thirty-three.

I remember his face from a newspaper clipping, his blond hair cut close. I imagine him with blue eyes. Cold blue eyes. Then I think that I don't know for sure. His eyes could have been grey or green. I imagine him climbing the steps of the tower. I wish I knew what he was thinking on that day. It could have been thoughts of death as he looked down on the campus or perhaps nothing at all, a seamless grey blankness inside his head where the autopsy discovered a tumor. A madman? I like to think of him as a miner's bird in a cage, his madness a warning to us all.

The Marines taught him to shoot. During the Vietnam war he was held up as a model for Marine recuits. Although I wasn't out to hurt anyone, I would've been more successful if I'd had a few lessons.

Alice names some movie she knows I've probably not been to see and waits for me to lie and say I have.

"I've got a better idea," I say.

"What's that?" Alice asks.

I look around the bar. There're ten people: three from the newpaper, the cop, a man and a woman sitting at a table, and four men who haven't bothered to take off their hard hats. The construction workers are on lunch break from the new building going up down the street. I calculate how much it's going to cost.

"Suzy, a round of beer for everyone," I say. "On me."

Suzy looks at me like I've gone crazy.

"What?" Suzy asks.

"Hunter, hush," Alice says.

The cop turns and looks at me, the leather of his pistol belt creaking. This year the force all got nine millimeter automatics. The pistol rests encased in the black leather, the bluing perfect. If it were mine, I'd have walnut grips on it instead of those cheap plastic ones.

"I mean it," I say. "A Dixie beer for everyone."

The construction workers look at Suzy. They want their beer before I change my mind. The newspaper people, two young women and an older man, look at each other and laugh.

"The money first," Suzy says.

I put a fifty-dollar bill on the counter. It's the last of my unemployment money. The cop stares at it. I suppose he's wondering if it's counterfeit.

Suzy takes the bill and makes change, which she counts out to me on the bartop. Alice starts to pick it up, but I stop her. I want them to think another round might be coming if they stay and listen.

"I am the Ole Miss Sniper," I begin.

The cop has got a smile on his face. He's probably anticipating putting the cuffs on me. It'll be easy for him. His arms fill up the sleeves of his uniform.

Then I realize the cop is too young to have heard of what I did. I look at the construction workers, but they're all too young. I've waited too late to tell it.

"I covered that story for *Commercial Appeal*," the newspaper man says. "It was sixty-eight."

I'm thankful he's here. That he knows.

"Sixty-seven," I say.

He looks up at the ceiling and pauses.

"Yeah, it was sixty-seven," he says. "I must be getting old."

The two women laugh.

"I took my grandfather's octagonal barrel .22 up to Ole Miss to use for squirrel hunting," I say. "It was a lever action, a fine old rifle. I'd helped him refinish the walnut stock. He'd had the barrel and receiver reblued."

Alice puts her hand on my shoulder. She begins to rub it. But she doesn't say anything.

"We were sitting around the Sigma Chi house one night," I say. "Somebody bet me I couldn't shoot out the light on the water tower."

I explain to them how the water tower was set on a hill above the men's dormitories. Behind it was a ravine filled with oak and kudzu.

"I walked up fraternity row and then behind the student health center and the university laundry and then down into the ravine. I'd taken a box of shells. It took me a long time to find a place where I could get a clear view of that red light, but I finally did. I remember I was real worried about stepping on a snake."

"Suzy, give me another one," a construction worker says.

He's chug-a-lugged his. He's got a big smile on his face.

"Sure," I said. "Give it to him."

Suzy opens the beer and shoves it across the bar. He takes a sip and waits for me to continue. Having them listen is worth one more beer.

"I used a pine limb for a rest and started shooting. I guess I shot a round every five seconds or so. I was trying to shoot it out in less than ten shots. But pretty soon the magazine was empty, and I had to reload. Then I shot faster, because I wanted to knock out the light before someone came to investigate the sound of the shooting.

"What I didn't know was that the rounds were ricocheting off the tower and hitting the men's dorm across the street. And I didn't know, as I shot the last of the box of shells, that the campus police were lying on the grass in front of the dorm, shotguns and pistols ready, searching the tower for the sniper.

"People at Ole Miss were edgy then. There'd been riots when the federal government forced the university to accept James Meredith, the first black student at a Mississippi school. Just a few years before, the woods beside the tower were filled with federal troops on bivouac. Their camp was surrounded by concertina wire. And there was the Texas Tower Sniper.

"I ran out of ammuntion and put the rifle over my shoulder and walked back to the fraternity house. I didn't find out what happened until we turned on the ten o'clock news. Nobody got hurt, just a couple of broken windows."

The construction worker finishes his second beer in one long swallow and sets the mug on the counter.

"You were a lucky son of a bitch," he says.

"But I was left with what to do with the rifle," I say. "I drove out to the Tallahatchie River. By the time I got there it was almost midnight. I parked my car and walked out on the bridge and dropped the rifle in the river."

I don't tell them about how bad dropping the rifle made me feel. I stood on the bridge for a long time with the rifle in my hands and the longer I stood the heavier it felt. I remembered my grandfather placing it in my hands and telling me it was mine. Then a set of headlights appeared at the top of the hill leading down into the river bottom and I let it go. It made a splash but a smaller one than I had expected. I stood and looked down at the water I couldn't see.

"I bet you forgot to wipe your prints off it," the cop said.

"No, I did that," I said.

"Smarter than you look," the cop said.

Everyone laughs. Alice rubs the back of my neck.

"That rifle is probably still there," I say.

I feel foolish now. Alice had tried to shut me up, but I hadn't listened. The people from the newspaper crowd around me. I tell them my name.

"Does your father know about this?" the newspaper man says.

My daddy, Effington Drayton, is still practicing law in his father's law offices. Everyone on the coast knows him.

Then the reporters get interested in my getting fired from the paper company. But when they find out I was in management and have no tales of chemicals released into the river, they lose interest. After the reporters leave, the construction workers go back to their job. The cop thanks me for the beer and walks out. The couple at the table, who never stopped drinking bourbon and coke, ignore us.

"Honey, are you all right?" Alice asks.

"Fine," I say.

We have a few more beers and then go to a movie I've already seen twice. Alice likes to go to movies on weekday afternoons when most people are working.

Afterwards we buy some fried chicken and go to her apartment and watch another movie on her VCR. Then we make love. About ten o'clock, the last of a pitcher of vodka martinis on the seat between us, we arrive at the beach with our flounder spears and headlamps.

Out in the water we can see the lights of other flounder hunters. It's still hot. We wade into the warm knee-deep water. There are no waves. The Gulf is like a huge puddle of water spread out before us. For waves you have to go out to the barrier islands. The channel is a quarter of a mile away. The water will not rise to more than waist deep until we reach it.

"What are you going to do?" Alice asks.

"I don't know," I say.

She could have asked me that question a hundred times but had to wait until we were out in the water. Everything can wait until we're through hunting flounder.

"You should have a plan," she says.

I look past her at the sweep of the lights on the shore, the neon pulsing blue and gold and red in the signs marking the motels and bars. I look at the stream of headlights on the highway. And beyond that hysterical blaze of color the soft glow of the lights from the suburbs. Out to sea it's dark except for a few buoy lights and far out what are probably the lights of a tanker.

"Maybe I'll buy myself a scuba outfit," I say. "Go up and dive for granddaddy's rifle."

I imagine it lying covered with rust on the bottom of the river. I want her to ask me why I want to do that, but she says nothing.

Instead, Alice peers down into the water. Then she jabs at something with her spear. She curses.

"A big one," she says.

I concentrate on fishing and hope she won't talk anymore. Alice likes to talk. She carries on conversations while we make love. Today she talked about the movie. It can be disconcerting, but I've gotten used to it.

"You won't be able to pay your rent," she says.

"I've been thinking about going to work on a shrimp boat," I say.

"You'll get seasick."

She's beginning to remind me of my father. She has an answer for everything.

"I know," I say.

I look out at the red light on a buoy and think of my performance in the bar. My family is not going to be happy when they read about it in the paper.

"Well?" she says.

Her headlamp sweeps across my face, temporarily blinding me.

"I'm having flounder and grits for breakfast," I say.

I speak these words into darkness. Then the lights from the beach pop back into focus.

"Good," she says. "But if we had to depend on you, it'd be just grits every morning."

She's right. I'm a lousy flounder fisherman.

We walk slowly, perhaps ten yards apart, like two great herons fishing the shallows.

I concentrate and fish hard but have no luck. She spears a flounder and laughs at me. I put the fish in a net bag I carry over my shoulder. We walk several hundred yards before she spears another one. This time she doesn't laugh. I haven't even seen a flounder.

"We should go back," she says.

"Why?" I ask.

"It's hot. The fish will spoil."

"I don't think so."

She may be right, but I want to stay out in that warm, dark water. We could fill the net with flounder before morning. They'd be worth something. I imagine the money piling up. I imagine myself starting a business.

"Let's go back," she says.

She speaks so softly I can barely hear the words.

I look at the beach and try to pick out her car but can't find it. We parked under a streetlight, the mercury vapor lamp making my white shirt look purple. She puts her arms around me. Our headlamps get in the way so we take them off.

She tastes salty and smells of perfume and fish. My head feels very clear. And I can feel her body in a way I've never felt it before. As I run my hands over her hips, I imagine the muscles and bone that lie beneath. It's going to be a long time before I find another woman like her. I wonder if I'm thinking this because I'm getting ready to leave. But how can I leave a place where I've lived until middle age?

"Hunter, why did you tell that story?" she asks.

"I don't know," I say.

"Did you make it up?"

"No."

I think that it might have been better for me if I'd made it up. Then the whole affair wouldn't have the aspect of a confession. For some reason I think of St. Augustine. I read his book a couple of months ago.

"I want you to promise me you'll shave off that beard and go look for a job," she said. "I don't care if you have to work in New Orleans or Mobile or even Atlanta. We can see each other on weekends."

This takes me by surprise. Now she is going to make it easy to leave. I don't like problems that have easy solutions.

"I told you," I say. "I'm going to work on a shrimp boat."

"The season is almost over," she says. "They won't hire you. And you can't read on a shrimp boat."

She is laughing now. Her not taking me seriously offends something in me. Then I consider whether it's Alice who is getting ready to leave. That's why she wants me installed in a new job. New York might be better than Atlanta.

I think of these things as we start back to the beach. I turn and look out to sea. The lights of the tanker have disappeared. There're only the buoys, whose red lights remind me of the eyeshine of spotlighted alligators, and the lights of the other flounder hunters. The night sky, the edge out to sea sprinkled with stars, seems too high, as if the fabric holding them together has torn, sky and sea drifting away from each other.

Alice stands just out of my reach. Her headlamp sweeps the water. I turn my lamp off. She stops and stands and looks at me. Then with a smooth casual motion, as if she were arranging her hair, she reaches up and switches her light off. As we both stand in the darkness, I think how we're invisible to anyone watching from the beach.

We don't say anything because there's nothing to say. I move toward her, the warm water swirling about my knees. I take her hand. We stand there, our faces turned toward the beach, toward that festival of lights, holding hands in the dark.

THE HORSE TRAINER'S WIFE

Debbie stood before the full length mirror and examined her body. Her breasts were beginning sag. She sucked in her stomach and turned slowly about. She was thankful there was no hint of varicose veins in her legs. Her mother's legs had been crisscrossed with what she and her sister called "blue worms." She took a pinch of skin on her thigh between thumb and forefinger and let it snap back into place, reassured somewhat by its elasticity. But it wasn't the same as when she was eighteen. Then she had been perfect. Today she was thirty.

The vet's pickup had just come by the house, its tires rattling on the gravel. Jerry was already down at the barn with the horses. On the kitchen table downstairs were the wrapping paper and a ribbon, the remains of her present. It had been a new sweater, now put away in the cedar chest in the bedroom.

She dressed slowly and then walked to the barn where she found them with one of the mares. The vet had pushed a yellow rubber tube up the mare's nostril and down her throat. Now he was pouring liquid into it through a funnel while Jerry held her head. The mare's eyes were rolled back, and she jerked her head as Jerry struggled to hold her.

"Worms," Jerry said.

She left them and went back to the house, not wanting to watch their brutal way with the mare. She threw away the wrapping paper but saved the ribbon and bow. Then she spent the rest of the morning washing clothes and ironing Jerry's shirts. She worked in a kind of mindless rhythm, listening to the music on the radio, and sometimes singing along.

Then it was lunchtime, and she knew he'd probably invite the vet to eat with them. She went about the kitchen preparing the meal, moving still as if she were in a dream. She reached into the cabinet for a can of soup and found herself wondering if she might be able to pass her hand through it. Later she found herself standing in the center of the kitchen not thinking at all. She heard the sound of the soup boiling and went to take it off the stove.

As she expected, he brought the vet in for lunch. They came in with faces and hands red from the cold, their boots caked with dark mud from the barn and paddock. Soon the kitchen floor was covered with mud. She thought of sending them out to take off the boots but decided to say nothing. Perhaps she'd scold Jerry tomorrow after the birthday was over.

Both men were pleased over the worming, self-satisfied with the job they'd done. The vet was a small, dark-haired man who moved with quick certainty about the horses.

"Have you started the cake yet?" Jerry asked.

"No," she said. "I will after lunch."

"We wormed 'em," Jerry said. "Jack found they all needed it, just like I thought."

Jack smiled in agreement.

"I'll bet you'll be taking Debbie to the Wagon Wheel to go dancing," Jack said.

It was a nightclub in Birmingham. Debbie liked to dance. Jerry was a clumsy dancer.

"No," Jerry said. "We'll stay home and sit by the fire. Have a few drinks. Debbie don't want to go to Birmingham."

She thought of sitting in a restaurant he had once taken her to. They'd had wine with dinner. The whole time Jerry had been uncomfortable.

"Cost you a week's pay to eat at one of those fancy restaurants," Jack said. "Food's not much good anyhow."

She could tell that Jack was embarrassed, but Jerry didn't notice. He just went on talking.

"I'm going to make an addition to the barn," he said. "I'm going to put in some more stalls and maybe add a room on one end. It'll be insulated so I could sleep out there if I had to in cold weather. It'd be good for foaling time. You know, I might even put in a wood-burning stove."

The men began to talk eagerly about the plans for the barn. She went to the stove to finish preparing the food. This was the first she'd heard about an addition to the barn. She wondered where the money would come from. He had worked at one of the steel mills in Birmingham as a production line supervisor, but now he'd been laid off. He didn't seem to be worried about it, for he joked to all his friends that he was on vacation. It was uncertain when he would return.

He'd inherited the farm from his father. They could count on some money from the land he rented out, but there'd not be enough to pay for the house and the vehicles and now an addition to the barn. He made no money from the horses; they were a hobby. He liked to take them to shows. She'd watch from the grandstand while he rode in competition. He was very good at it, and she liked to see him sitting tall and straight on his favorite horse, a big white stallion. She liked to ride, but not in shows.

Once the food was on the table, she sat and watched the men eat. She wasn't hungry. Their talk continued about the addition to the barn. That would mean more horses, more business for the vet.

When they finished eating, he went out of the house with the vet, who had to leave to make another call. She started to work on the cake. Now she wished that he'd bought her one in town. But she knew he'd never think of that. Once the cake was in the oven, she cleaned the mud off the kitchen floor, growing angry as she worked. She decided to go to Birmingham the next day and visit one of the colleges there. She'd been thinking about going to school for a long time.

He'd disapprove of her plan; he was perfectly satisfied with the way things were. Perhaps she'd become a teacher. She might be able to get a job with the county system or in one of the nearby towns.

Once the cake was finished and iced, she started a fire in the fireplace, sat by it, and read a magazine. She wondered if it would have been different if they'd had children. They'd been married five years now. He wanted children, sons, but she'd refused, and that was always just beneath the surface, ready to flare up at any moment. She'd wondered from time to time if not wanting children meant that something was wrong with her. Her mother, who had brought her to Alabama from Texas when Debbie was fourteen, had expected her to have children. Now her mother was dead.

He took a neighbor's children, who lived on a farm a few miles down the road, hunting and fishing and to horse shows. Their father, a pilot, had been killed in Vietnam—not really killed for sure, but missing and presumed dead. The widow, a frail, nervous woman, had moved in with her parents. She'd visited the woman a few times but soon gave up the possibility of establishing a friendship with her. That left her isolated and alone. Jerry's parents had moved to Florida. Her friends from high school were busy raising their children.

Jerry came back into the house. Leaving the fire, she went into the kitchen. He was taking off his coat and hanging it up on the rack by the door. He carried himself very straight and erect, as if he expected an assault to be made on him at any moment. She pictured him playing high school football. He'd run into the line, holding the ball firmly tucked under one arm, with the same straight-up style. He'd told her his coach always complained that it was an unsuitable way to run and exposed him to tackles.

"Where're the candles?" he asked.

"We don't have any," she said.

He kissed her.

"Sure we do," he said.

"No, I looked," she said.

Now he was searching the cupboard, and she found herself growing angry.

"I know where," he said as he left the room.

He returned a few moments later with a box of candles.

"I put 'em in the den after my birthday," he said. "How many do you want to use?"

She didn't reply.

"We'll put in eighteen," he said.

He looked at her and laughed.

"Put them all," she said.

There was a taste like metal in her mouth.

"If there are fifty put them all."

He laughed again, not seeing her anger and despair.

"I need to go to town," she said.

"Aw, Debbie, I was just teasing," he said.

"I'm going."

Now he was angry, and she was afraid of him. She didn't like to anger him. He'd never struck her, but she'd seen him beat a man once who tried to cheat him over a horse sale. She believed that Jerry would have killed him if the other men hadn't pulled him off. His easygoing nature was a cover for something ugly, black, and violent.

"Well, go then," he said.

He got up and put on his coat. Then he went out of the house. Through the window she saw him heading for the barn. When she went out the door to the car, he was riding across the pasture, sitting straight and tall on the big white stallion.

By the time she reached town, she was sorry for the way she'd treated him. She bought a pair of shoes at a shop and went to the post office to check their mailbox. Then she started home. It was now mid-afternoon and she was hungry. Near the edge of town was a barbecue stand. "Quick Pig" was written on the side of a huge plastic pig set on the roof. She and

Jerry had explored each other's bodies there on Saturday nights in his car parked under the locust trees.

She went inside. The jukebox was playing much too loud, and there were kids in the booths along the walls. A few of them stared at her for a moment before returning their attention to their food or friends. When her barbecue was ready, she decided to eat it in the car. She got into the car and opened the sack.

"Be cool, lady," the voice said, a thin, high-pitched one. She felt something hard and cold against the back of her neck. "If you scream or do anything, I'll blow your brains all over the windshield."

She looked up into the rearview mirror. He was young, like the kids inside, his long blond hair held back with a headband.

"Drive out of here," he said.

She started the car and put it in gear.

"Go out on the highway, away from town," he said.

"Let me out," she said. "You can have the car."

She was surprised she could even talk.

"Shut up and drive," he said.

They left the town behind them, the highway running straight through hills covered with pines. The road was deserted. She wondered how she could attract someone's attention when a car did appear. Maybe she could turn the lights on without his noticing and flash them.

"What do you want?" she asked.

"You," he said.

His voice was deeper now, more confident.

She started to scream, but through an effort of will managed not to. Still there was no traffic on the road. As she went down a hill, she saw the red-tipped needle on the speedometer gradually climb to seventy-five.

"Slow down," he said.

Treble was in his voice again.

She laughed and pressed down harder on the accelerator. The needle climbed to eighty-five.

"I'll blow your brains out," he said. "I mean it."

There was a desperate, broken tone in his voice now. The needle quivered on ninety. The car made a huge rushing sound between the walls of pines.

"Go ahead, kill me," she said. "I'm thirty today. My life is over."

"Stop the goddamn car!" he screamed.

The gun barrel pressed hard against the back of her neck. It was then that she realized she wished he'd kill her. She pressed the accelerator all the way to the floor. The car was heavy and powerful, and it was not until this moment that she'd felt a real sensation of speed. She almost forgot about the boy with the gun as she watched the road rushing up to meet them. This was the first time she'd driven so fast. Now she felt the car begin to vibrate a little, and every time they crested a hill she expected they'd leave the road and sail off into the pines.

"Throw the gun out and I'll stop," she said.

She liked the sound of her voice. It was strong and even.

"I'll kill you!" he screamed. "I'll kill you!"

She laughed.

"You'll be doing me a favor," she said.

He was silent. The heavy sound of his breathing was in her ear.

"OK," he said. "OK."

He rolled down the window, a great rush of cold air filling the car. She was afraid she'd lose control. She let up on the accelerator a little.

"Throw it where I can see," she said.

In the rearview mirror she saw the gun flash in the sunlight as it sailed through the air, hit the road, and bounced off the pavement and into a ditch. At the crest of a hill she pulled the car off the road onto a patch of gravel.

"Get out," she said.

He slid across the seat and opened the door. Then he was standing on the gravel.

"Don't tell—" he began.

But the rest of his words were lost, for she'd pressed the accelerator to the floor. The tires spun in the gravel, and the car fishtailed out onto the road, the open door slamming shut as the car straightened itself. In the rearview mirror she saw him shielding his eyes from the dust. Then he disappeared from view, a forlorn figure standing by the side of the highway.

When she got home, she said nothing of her experience to Jerry. She hadn't even cried afterwards. She'd driven along, one hand on the wheel, and held out her free hand to see if it was shaking. But it wasn't. It was as steady as a rock. She felt strong and renewed.

Jerry cooked steaks on the patio. Afterwards she lit the candles on the cake. There were eighteen of them. His idea. They sat by the fire in the den and drank whiskey.

Then they went to the bedroom and made love. Jerry was never very good in bed. She had given up counting on much from him and knew that it would be over quickly. And if he couldn't he might smash his fist into the wall or knock a lamp off a bedside table. She dreaded those rages, so she handled him gently, running her hands along his back, talking soothingly to him in the way he liked, bringing him to the end. Afterwards he slept.

She crept out of bed and went into the den. The bottle was still half full. She poured herself a drink and then another. As the sun started to come up she was still drinking, the events of the day before giving her a kind of immunity to the whiskey. She still had that strong and confident feeling and she wanted to nurture it, feared that it might be lost in sleep. Once the sun cleared the tops of the pines at the end of the pasture, she went to bed.

It was midday when she got up. Her head felt clear, and she wondered if she was still drunk. She waited for the hangover to come, but instead felt better as the day progressed. All afternoon she saw little of him. He stayed down at the barn with the horses. Late that afternoon, after he returned from a trip to town, he came into the kitchen where she was frying chicken.

"I saw Shaw at the hardware store," he said. "He told me you came by him yesterday on the highway. He was there at the stop sign on the Cane road. Said you must've been doing a hundred, and there was someone in the back seat of the car."

"It was somebody else," she said.

She felt no fear of him and was surprised at herself for being able to calmly deny it.

He seemed confused, but she saw that he'd decided to believe her.

"I wonder who it was he saw?" he said.

He put on his coat and went out the door. She shrugged her shoulders and began to turn the chicken, the grease hissing in the iron skillet.

Just after Thanksgiving she drove the eighty miles to Birmingham to visit a college. She and Jerry had been arguing about the idea for weeks. Again, like so many times when they'd quarreled, he retreated to the barn, where one end had the naked studs nailed up marking the beginning of the addition, and saddled the big white stallion. She hated even to look at the addition, for it represented the money he'd borrowed from the bank and, since he was still without a job, had no way of paying back. The bank would end up with the farm. He was angry because she'd asked him to borrow money for her tuition. As she drove away from the house, she watched him riding the big horse across the pasture toward the green wall of pines which marked the beginning of the national forest. When they'd fought over money, he'd told her that he intended to make a living training and breeding horses.

When she came out of the hills and down into the bowl-shaped depression that held the city, there was a yellowish haze from the steel mills in the air. She hated the city, yet here would be her escape.

All morning and part of the afternoon she spent talking with admissions officers and taking a tour of the campus. Then, with a stack of registration forms on the front seat beside her, she started out of town. Ahead, over the tops of the buildings, she could see the hills where the air was clean.

He came into her field of vision unexpectedly as if this were the dream she'd never yet had of him. He was standing on a street corner waiting for the light to change. He looked just like he had when she'd left him on the highway, his blond hair in a tangle and an air of confusion about him. He'd now fixed his eyes on the sidewalk as if he were thinking deeply about something.

The light changed before she reached the corner, and he started across the street. She drove past him and parked by the curbside to watch him approach the rearview mirror. As he passed, she slid across the seat, knocking the forms onto the floor, and rolled down the window.

"Hey," she said.

He stopped and turned.

"Remember me?" she asked. And quickly added, "Don't run. I didn't tell anyone."

For a moment he had the furtive look of a startled deer. Then he swaggered over to her, his head held high. Now she wondered what she was going to say, but could think of nothing.

"Get in," she said.

He opened the door, and she slid back over to the driver's side. As she drove out into the traffic, he began to pick up the forms and stack them on the seat.

"Are you going to school?" he asked.

"I'm thinking about it," she said.

She thought this was like the awkwardness of a blind date. She started to laugh but checked herself. He would think she was laughing at him.

"I go to night school at the University," he said. "I'm on the G.I. Bill."

"You look too young to have been in Vietnam," she said.

He stiffened and glared at her.

"I'm twenty-two," he said. "I know how old you are."

"I'm sorry," she said.

There was an awkward silence.

"What are you studying?" she asked.

"Engineering," he said. "But I ain't doing too good. I mean it's really that I don't like it that much. I've been thinking about going into business administration, or maybe computer science. Yeah, computer science, that's where it's at."

She turned off the street onto a ramp leading up to the interstate.

"Why did you pick me up?" he asked.

"I don't know," she said.

"I wasn't gonna hurt you that day. Would you've really driven the car off the road?"

"Yes."

"I don't believe that."

"You believed it that day."

He stared out the window. She'd hurt his pride. Now he reminded her of Jerry.

"Are you taking me home with you?" he asked.

"No, I can't do that," she said.

He hesitated. She was changing lanes.

"If you take the next exit, we can go to my place," he said.

She didn't reply, but when the exit appeared she took it. They were in an older residential section of the city. Now he became more talkative as if he felt secure on his home ground. He told her his name was Percy Loam. She told him she thought it was a nice name.

The neighborhood was in a state of decay, the old two-story houses in need of paint and repair. Many of the houses had been torn down and replaced by office buildings or apartments. He told her to stop in front of a large Victorian.

"I got me a room on the third floor," he said. "It's up in the turret."

She followed him up a flight of outside stairs to the second floor. Now she was a little afraid. They went into the house and along a hall to another flight of stairs that led up to the turret room.

There was no furniture in the room, only a mattress on the floor. Scattered about the room were books, magazines, records, and dirty clothes. A stereo was set up on the floor, the speakers in the windows.

"Things are in kind of a mess," he said.

He gathered up an armful of dirty clothes and threw them in the closet.

"Do you live here alone?" she asked.

"Yeah, most of the time," he said.

So far she'd played the role of leader, but now she was unsure what to do next. Instead of taking the initiative, he continued to talk. He was describing the parties he'd held in the turret room. Suddenly she felt very tired. She sat down on the sheetless mattress. A sleeping bag was rolled up in a corner. The radiators ticked. It was too warm in the room. She imagined him lying alone on the mattress beneath the naked light bulb, smoking while he looked at pictures of cars or foldouts of naked girls.

He sat down beside her.

"I was having a barbecue when I saw you come in," he said. "I was hitch-hiking through. I guess I kind of fell in love with you."

She felt like laughing out loud but checked herself. The radiators continued to tick. She examined the mattress, which appeared to be clean. He'd put a cigarette in his mouth and began looking through his pockets for matches. She took him by the shoulder, his flesh feeling thin over the bones, and pulled him down on the mattress. As they took off their clothes, she marvelled at how smooth and white his skin was. She ran her hand over his back.

"There's not a mark on you," she said.

She'd expected him to be scarred by a bullet or a knife.

"Sure there is," he said.

He pointed out a spot on his arm. There was a reddish raised welt.

"Piece of schrapnel nicked me," he said. "Got me a Purple Heart."

She pulled him down on top of her. He was clumsy and moved too fast. She slowed him down.

"I'm used to them other girls," he said. "I—"

She put her hand over his mouth.

"Hush," she said.

He was young and eager. And there amid the tick of the radiators, the room like a hothouse, the mattress smelling of cigarettes, she coaxed him into a rhythm that suited her.

He got up and stood with his back to her, looking out one of the uncurtained windows.

"I didn't have anything to worry about that day," she said. "You might have killed me, but not raped me."

He recoiled at her words, taking a step backwards.

"You don't have no right to say that," he said.

"No one has more of a right than me," she said.

She felt giddy with the power she had over him. When she left the room, he was still standing by the radiator, that furtive deer-like quality on him again.

Jerry's truck was gone. When she got out of the car, she heard the snorts of the horses from the paddock that adjoined the barn. He didn't usually leave them free to roam there at night. She went down to the barn.

They were all in the pen: the big stallion, three mares, and the gelding. Led by the stallion, they ran in circles about the paddock, their tails and manes flying in the light of the half moon.

Opening the gate, she went inside the paddock. The horses retreated to a corner and regarded her warily, their ears twisting about. Then one of the mares she often rode trotted over to her and pushed its wet nose into her hand in search of the apple she sometimes brought with her. She took the mare by the halter and led her into the barn, the others following except for Traveler, the stallion. After she'd put the horses in their stalls and fed them, she returned to the paddock to find the stallion trotting in circles with his tail held high. She tried to drive him into the barn, but he refused to enter. Finally he stood in the center of the paddock and allowed her to approach. She thought she'd be able to walk up to him and take hold of the halter, but when she came within arm's reach of it, he stamped his foot and shook his head. For the first time she was afraid of him. Then he bolted past her, his huge body coming so close she felt the wind of its passing on her face. She went out of the paddock and watched him trot in circles.

"I'm not afraid of you, you big bastard," she said.

The stallion snorted and tossed his head. She returned to the house and went to sleep.

She received a scholarship from the college. It came as a surprise. She read the letter on her way back from the mailbox, standing there on the gravel, the envelope torn out of her hands by the cold wind and tumbling across the pasture. She couldn't quite believe the words on the paper were real.

The winter quarter started, and she began to attend classes. She saw Percy again from time to time but didn't sleep with him again. They had coffee once. He asked her back to his apartment but she refused. He seemed hurt; she was sorry for that.

But her plans for the future took all her attention. She was going to finish her degree and leave Jerry. The idea of a new life somewhere filled her with excitement.

One day she came home very late; she'd been busy with work at the library. As she drove home, she thought of how angry he'd be over having to fix his own supper.

The sheriff's car was parked in the driveway. She didn't think there was anything unusual about that. The sheriff had gone to high school with Jerry, and they were great friends. She saw them walking up to the house from the barn.

"They got 'em all," Jerry said.

Thompson, the sheriff, hung back behind him.

She had never seen Jerry so upset. He waved his arms about and his face was red.

"They took 'em all," he said.

He was shouting. Then he calmed some.

"They cut the pasture fence," he said. "Used apples. Ben found a core on the ground. If you, if you—"

He turned away from her in rage and stalked into the house.

"It ain't your fault," Thompson said. "If you'd been here, you might have gotten hurt."

"Will you catch them?" she asked.

"Probably not. We ain't caught a one of 'em yet. They're real slick."

She felt sorry for Jerry, but was secretly glad the horses were gone. Now he'd find a job.

But she soon discovered he had no intention of finding a job. He stayed away from the house, sometimes for days at a time. And when he was home she knew the anger was just beneath the surface, ready to flame over her. She was afraid and therefore careful. She didn't question him. She was sure it wasn't another woman. Whatever he was doing she was certain it was not bringing him any pleasure. Finally, though, she had to ask.

"I've been going to horse sales," he said. "If those bastards are stupid enough to sell Traveler in Mississippi, Alabama, or Tennessee, I'll catch 'em."

He pulled back his coat to show her the pistol in the shoulder holster.

"Please don't kill anyone," she said.

"They won't get away with what's mine," he said.

"They probably went up North with them."

He sighed.

"You're most likely right," he said. "I've about decided to give up. I'm going to buy new stock. We need to hire someone to watch the place while we're gone. Is your cousin Steve still out of work?"

"No, he went back last week."

She wanted to ask him where the money was coming from but was afraid it would anger him.

"I'll put an ad in the paper," he said.

Then he went off to work on the barn.

The next day, when her classes were over, she returned to the car to find a note from Percy under the windshield wiper. Lately he'd been leaving her notes almost every day. He wanted her to meet him at The Tombs, a bar near the school. Today, she thought, she'd put an end to the notes. She'd tell him that she wanted him to stay away from her.

At The Tombs, which was built below street level, she found him at a table with a half-empty glass of beer before him. He looked bad; he was dirty and had the beginnings of a thin blond beard. When she sat down, he barely acknowledged her presence.

"I spent the last of my money on this beer," he said.

She took a five dollar bill out of her purse and shoved it across the table.

"This is the first and last of it," she said. "You can pay me back when you get your loan money."

"They won't let me have it," he said.

He still hadn't touched the money.

"Why?" she asked.

She was irritated because she was being drawn into a conversation she hadn't intended to have.

"My grades," he said. "You gotta have a C average. I don't. I would've except for that Dr. Bradley don't like me."

"Go home."

"I can't. Like I told you they threw me out. Sometimes, you know, I think maybe I'm dying of something like cancer. Some days we'd walk around in the jungle, and they'd be dropping that Agent Orange on us."

"Can't you stay with friends?"

"Don't have any."

"You'll have to get a job," she said. "I'll give, not lend, you enough for a few days."

"No."

"What do you want then?"

"I love you."

He looked down at the table.

"I don't love you," she said slowly and plainly so he'd not fail to understand. "I don't love anyone."

"But you're married?"

"Love isn't a part of that."

"Why'd you have to bother me? You could've just kept right on driving down the street. You could've called the cops."

"That's enough. You're going to go home and get yourself cleaned up. And sleep. You look like you need to sleep. You'll feel better then."

"No, I can't."

She wanted to get up and walk out but found she couldn't.

"My husband might give you a job," she said.

She wondered why she hadn't thought of this before. Jerry would be paying someone who'd threatened one of his possessions. It would be a great joke on him.

"Doing what?" he asked.

"Looking after horses on our farm," she said. "We had some horses stolen. He'd probably want you to sleep out in the barn. One of the rooms is insulated. It'd be OK with your sleeping bag."

"I'd like that."

"I'll talk to my husband and let you know tomorrow."

"Can't I come today? I ain't got a place to sleep."

She started to say no, but changed her mind. This way Jerry would have to let him work at least one day.

"You'll have to get yourself cleaned up," she said. "He won't hire you the way you look. You'll have to cut your hair."

Percy ran his hands through the tangle of his hair.

"I don't mind," he said.

She gave him money to buy shaving gear and a change of clothes. He got his hair cut. Then he went to one of the dormitories on campus and took a shower and shaved. When he appeared at the bar again, his hair was cut almost military short. She liked the way he looked. He could have been one of those boys who took her out in high school.

Once they were out of the city, he leaned back against the seat and went to sleep. They were close to the farm when he woke up.

"How much do you think he'll pay me?" he asked.

"Not much, but you'll get your meals and a place to sleep," she said.

"Yeah, I could save up and go back to school. I think I'll change my major back to business again."

Jerry wasn't home, but she installed Percy in the barn anyway. She hung a note on both the barn and kitchen doors informing Jerry that she'd hired a boy to look after the horses.

In the morning when she woke, she heard Jerry in the kitchen. She found him sitting at the table drinking coffee.

"I shot that boy you hired," Jerry said. "Thought he was a horse thief."

He began to laugh.

She wondered what kind of expression had appeared on her face, as for a moment she had believed him.

"Then we'll never be able to get any help," she said, trying to appear as indifferent as possible.

"Where'd you find him?" he asked.

"At school. He needs a job and will work cheap. That's what you want, isn't it?"

"Yeah, cheap is right. But will he work?"

"If he doesn't, you can fire him."

"Good then. I've been looking around for weeks and ain't found anyone. Nobody knows how to work anymore."

To her surprise, Percy turned out to be a good worker. She discovered he could cook, in fact liked to cook, and she persuaded Jerry to let him cook breakfast for them. That allowed her to sleep an extra half hour. After this proved a success, he was given the job of preparing dinner. He never left the farm, and she assumed he was doing this to save money for school.

There were plenty of horses for Percy to guard. Jerry had been steadily buying stock. Two of the mares were pregnant. He hoped to sell the foals for a good price, and this, along with the rent from the land when the crop was made in the fall, would help to pay off part of their debt at the bank.

She began to make love to Percy in the barn. The first time it took her by surprise. Jerry was gone to a horse sale, and she, exhausted from studying, wandered down to the barn to talk with Percy. They made love in an empty foaling stall. It was the texture of the straw under her legs and back, the smell of the horses and the woodburning stove, and his youth that she liked. She couldn't draw close to him at all. And he wanted love.

"I love you," he had said.

She wanted him to be quiet.

"Let's not talk of love," she said.

"Then why did you come down here?" he asked.

She ran her hands over his back and then along the schrapnel scar on his arm.

"I hate my husband," she said.

She didn't think she was doing it for that, but here was something he could understand.

"I still love you," he said.

And there was no real reply she could make to that, because she had come to him.

"Don't," she said. "Don't say that to me again. I won't come here again if you do."

But she found herself returning to the barn every time Jerry was gone. Percy never talked of love again. He told her about Vietnam and his childhood and his fears that he was dying.

Then it was spring. One of the cutting horses Jerry owned was winning races, and the barn filled with horses for him to train. It appeared that his business was going to prosper.

She had begun to make love to Percy when Jerry was there, though it really wasn't necessary. Jerry was gone much of the time. Jerry knew that something between them had changed. She could see it in his eyes when he looked at her over breakfast, like a horse catching a dangerous scent on the wind.

Yet she persisted and one day found herself lying in the hay with Percy while Jerry was working with a horse in the paddock. She imagined she could feel the vibration of the horses' hooves through the straw. A barn cat wandered through the stall. Percy shooed it away.

He didn't seem concerned about Jerry. He said they were safe as long as they heard the horse moving in the paddock. There'd be plenty of time to slip into their clothes.

She wasn't so sure. Jerry would kill him. It would be as simple as that. As they lay together on the straw, she felt that she had entered a labyrinth, a new word she'd learned at school, and was wandering in the darkness with no ball of string to follow to safety once the monster was slain. So she tried to envision the future, a time when she'd be completely free, like the stolen white stallion who could be ridden but never tamed. Jerry had said that once about the horse, that wildness was part of his value. But the future wouldn't come clear; the only definite things were the feel of the hay and the smell of the horses. It was all going to eventually come clear, she knew it would. She would wander through that world like a newborn foal across the new spring grass, wet and shining in the light, her legs growing stronger all the time.

THE MAGICIAN
AT THE NURSERY

Majorie took a step toward the field, one foot already out of the mown grass, but drew back. She was afraid of snakes. The boy was somewhere in the tall grass, the jungle, probably playing beneath the single sweet gum tree in the center of the field. Her fear of snakes was at once both reasonable and unreasonable. Anyone would hesitate before walking into an overgrown Mississippi field in July. But she couldn't bring herself to take the step, and most other people would, although they would be very careful.

"Jason, Jason," she called.

No answer, only the midsummer whine of insects. If she had a tractor and a bush-hog she could have cut the field in an hour, but she did not have a tractor or money to hire one. In one corner of the nursery where a row of holly bushes had died, tall stalks of Johnson grass had sprung up, their tasseled tops swaying in the breeze. That would have to be cut. She turned and walked along a pathway made out of wood chips, past rows of miniature fir trees, arborvitae, and variegated holly. Behind her she heard a rustling in the grass, and he walked out of the field.

"Didn't you hear me?" she asked.

"No, ma'am," he said.

"How could you not hear?"

"I was playing at the tree."

"You go do your watering."

She said nothing about snakes, not wishing to plant her fears on the child.

Jason trotted over to the office, a small prefabricated shed, and began connecting pieces of hose. Then he started watering a row of azaleas, the bushes protected from direct sunlight by a covering of green nylon mesh.

"Don't give them too much water," she yelled to him.

Jason looked up and smiled but continued pouring water on a plant.

"Jason, you'll drown them," she shouted.

He moved the hose away. Sometimes she thought she asked too much of Jason, who was only eight.

The nursery had been part of the divorce settlement. Majorie's husband had left Mississippi for good and gone off to Brazil to work on a deal that had something to do with importing knives or shotguns. She couldn't remember which. If the nursery failed, she would have to leave the small town, which was not quite close enough to Memphis to allow it to flourish, and return to school, maybe take an M.B.A. She was frustrated that her degree in marketing, which up to now she had never used, had not helped her in running the nursery, which had steadily lost money.

Mrs. Reed, who lived across the road, pointed out the nursery's failure to Majorie one day when they met at the mailboxes.

"Get your hair fixed pretty. Wear some lipstick. Won't be long before you have yourself a man," Mrs. Reed liked to say. "Let him worry about them plants."

Majorie replied, "I don't have time for men. I've got a business to run."

Mrs. Reed was suitably shocked, and Majorie was pleased. Majorie had gone out with a few men and even slept with one of them, but the ones she had met so far didn't seem worth the trouble. She had grown weary of doctors and lawyers, and even the art professor from Memphis State had turned out to be dull.

"Jason, you missed a bush," she shouted. "I know we're going to lose that one if you're not more careful."

I won't let this place fail, she thought. The plants will grow. I will sell them.

"Who's that man?" Jason asked.

She saw a man dressed in green work clothes standing in front of the office. At first she thought he was a customer but then noticed there was no car in the gravel parking lot.

Jason was out the door and talking to him before she could get out of the car. The man said something to make Jason laugh.

"Morning, ma'am," the man said, bowing slightly, a courtly gesture. "I'm Virgil Hoke."

His voice was deep and rich sounding with little hint of the sharp tones of a hillman in it. She imagined his father had been a sharecropper in the Delta.

He continued, "I was wondering if you needed any help around here?"

His black eyes were fixed on her, not set in the foxface of a hillman but in a round, smooth face that could have belonged to a banker.

"Ever worked in a nursery before?" she asked.

"No, ma'am," he said. "But I've farmed."

"What was your last job?"

"Planting pine trees," he said. "I didn't mind that. Then they gave me a killing tool. You stick it in a tree that's eat up with bugs and squeeze the handle to pump the poison in. Didn't like killing them trees."

"Business has not been good."

"I'll work for free for a bit. Just let me sleep in your office."

"Give him a job," Jason said, tugging at her arm.

"Hush, Jason," she said. Then she continued, "Why would you work for free? Nobody works for free."

"I want a chance to show you what I can do with plants," he said. He hesitated a moment. "I've been in the penitentiary."

"With a wall and guards?" Jason asked.

"Not exactly. It's a big farm," Virgil said.

She pulled Jason close to her.

"Go unlock the office," she said, handing him the key.

"Aw, Mom—" Jason began.

"Start the coffee," she said, giving him a push toward the steps.

Jason walked slowly, kicking at the gravel. She waited until he had opened the door and was inside the office before she spoke.

"I've got a little boy and—" She was furious with herself at her hesitation. Then she blurted it out, "What did you do?"

"Came home and found a man with my woman," he said. "I killed him. That's all. I'm out on parole. Down at Parchman I took care of the warden's yard. You'd of been proud to see it. Warden said he should've blocked my parole. Lost the best gardener he'd ever had."

He's telling tall tales, she thought. In a moment he would start laughing and announce he was one of Mrs. Reed's cousins.

"You'd work for free?" she asked, deciding to play his game.

"So I can show you what I can do. If you'll excuse me for saying so, them azaleas look a little sickly."

He took a card out of his pocket and handed it to her. It had the warden's name and telephone number printed on it.

So it was true. She was afraid, but irritated at herself for feeling fear. Jason came out of the office.

"Call him. He'll tell you I'm all right," Virgil said.

"I'll think about it," she said.

"Call him. I'll come back tomorrow."

He gave her a slight bow and patted Jason on the head. She watched him walk back out to the road.

"Are you going to hire him?" Jason asked.

"No," she said. "You go take a bag of fertilizer and a rake down to the roses. When you're through go cut the grass out of the old holly beds."

But that afternoon she made the long distance call to Parchman. She had to call three times before she found the warden in.

"Yes, I know Virgil," the warden said. "I gave him my card. You couldn't go wrong hiring him. I keep hoping he'll get in trouble again so they'll send him back."

The warden laughed and continued, "You won't have any trouble out of him. Murderers, especially if it's a crime of passion, get it out of their system once and for all. It's like they've used up all their meanness. Got none left over. And he makes things grow. Everything that man touches grows. I've lost three flowering plums since he's been gone. He's got more than a green thumb. That man's a real magician with plants."

When she hung up the phone, she was disgusted with herself for wasting money on the call. She would not hire the man. People would soon find out a convict was working for her, and that would be the end of her business.

The next morning when she went to work she found him standing in front of the office with the same self-assured manner. She wanted to be hostile toward him but found it impossible.

"Jason, go unlock the tool shed," she said, handing him the keys.

"Did you call the warden?" he asked, after Jason had left.

"Yes," she said.

"He said I was a good man?"

"Yes."

"Them azaleas. I'll fertilize them first."

He stood watching her with his black eyes. She looked at the plants arranged in rows beneath the screens, continually needing water, fertilizer, and fresh mulch. A crime of passion, the warden had said. The violence all drained out of him in one moment of anger. His gift could save the nursery.

"You can sleep in the office," she said, thinking she would have to remember to take the cash box home with her every night.

"Be right here all the time to take care of your place," he said.

"I'll be able to pay you when business improves."

Virgil looked toward the dying azaleas and said, "It'll pick up. You can count on that."

He thinks I'm a fool. Thinks I can't run this place, she thought. He'll find out it isn't so easy.

But he turned the azaleas from brown to green in only a few days. The warden had been right. Virgil had an almost magical way with plants. And he could sell them too. He liked to chat with customers about their purchases, something she had never been able to do.

Mrs. Reed was unimpressed.

"I wouldn't let that man take over my place," Mrs. Reed said, slamming her mailbox shut.

And when Majorie reminded her that Virgil was working for free, she laughed and said, "Oh, he ain't working for free, honey."

Majorie couldn't think of a retort so she just said goodbye to Mrs. Reed and walked off.

"He'll run everything," Mrs. Reed called after her.

Business improved, and she offered to pay him minimum wage.

"If that's what you want, ma'am," he said.

She said, "It's my nursery."

"I never said it wasn't, ma'am."

From the first Jason followed Virgil about the nursery. She no longer had to nag Jason to do his chores. Every day he begged her to let him stay longer so he could help Virgil with the plants. And Jason imitated Virgil's mannerisms. Jason now gave a slight bow to customers. Mrs. Reed thought it was cute. It was harmless, but Majorie wished Jason would stop.

"Virg's killed a snake!" Jason shouted.

She came out of the office. Virgil carried a headless snake draped over the end of a hoe. He dropped the snake on the ground and took out his knife.

"We're going to skin it. Make a hatband. It's a rattler," Jason said.

Virgil cut off the rattles and handed them to Jason. Jason shook the rattles, producing a dry, buzzing sound.

"I'll have that field cut," she said.

"I'll need a tractor," Virgil said.

"Burn it," she said.

Virgil said, "It's been dry. Could catch your place on fire. Frost'll be here soon. Run the snakes into their holes for the winter."

She went to the office to work on the books. When she went out to meet a customer, she saw them nailing up the skin on the side of the shed. They finished the job, and as they walked toward the office Jason mimicked the way Virgil walked, bouncing on the balls of his feet. Virgil and Jason reached the customer before she did, both man and boy making a slight bow.

I can make him go anytime I want, she thought, and felt better.

Jason called her to the telephone. It was Mrs. Reed.

"You know I usually mind my own business. But you've got to do something about that man who works for you," Mrs. Reed began.

"What's he done?" Majorie asked.

"He has women in your office every night. They run around outside half dressed. I've had about as much of it as I can stand."

Majorie asked, "Is a woman there tonight?"

"Why do you think I called?"

"I'll speak with him."

"When?" Mrs. Reed asked, the pitch of her voice rising.

"Tonight. Now," Majorie stammered into the telephone.

Jason wanted to go with her, but she left him in front of the TV after making him promise not to go outside. The nursery was less than a mile away. When she turned in the drive, she looked toward Mrs. Reed's house and saw her standing beneath the porch light.

The lights were on in the office. She slammed the car door hard to let them know she was there and walked slowly up to the door of the office. Just as she was putting the key to the lock, the door opened and Virgil stepped out into the darkness with her. He was barefoot, his shirt unbuttoned.

"Anything wrong, ma'am?" Virgil asked in a calm voice.

"I had a complaint," she said.

Virgil said, "We'll make it right. Don't want no dissatisfied customers."

"Get that woman out of my office," she said.

She found the sound of her own voice strange and hoped there was not a tremor in it. But if he heard and knew how nervous she was, he gave no sign.

He had begun to button up his shirt, and she saw his chest was hairless, smooth, his tanned skin shining in the light from the window.

She continued, "I want her off my property."

"That lady across the road has been making up lies," he said. "There ain't no woman in here."

He stepped away from the door, and she walked into the office. His air mattress was on the floor, and there was a nylon bag she had not seen before next to it. A plate with the remains of his supper was on the table.

And that was all. In five minutes his things could be cleared out, and it would be as if he had never existed. The thought of that made her sad.

She turned to face him.

"I'm sorry," she said.

He had stepped close to her, so close that she wanted to step back, put some distance between them, but she forced herself to stand her ground.

"I've been proud to work for you," he said.

Majorie thought how she wished there was someone to take over the business, someone to worry about the bills and the taxes and the cost of fertilizing and watering the plants.

"You worked hard," she said. "I—"

But what she was going to say, something about how embarrassed she was for invading his living space, escaped her. She reached out and put her hand on his chest, just below the second button on his shirt. She had not meant to put her hand there. It was like she was watching another woman do it. She felt the firm contours of muscle and bone.

When he took off his clothes, she expected there to be tattoos, or some scar from a knife or a bullet, but his skin was unmarked. He smelled of tobacco and a trace of whiskey. She expected he had a bottle hidden somewhere in the office.

Lying on the mattress, she felt his hands moving over her, the same hands which coaxed dying plants back to life. She didn't care that he had been in prison; she wasn't worried about the risk she was taking. This was not the same as going home with someone after a dance at the country club. Then he was inside her but moving too fast and it was over quickly. He apologized.

"It's been a long time for me," he said.

They lay on the mattress and drank from the bottle he had hidden in the filing cabinet. She felt comfortable with him in a way that she had not thought possible.

Jason's school started, and she was left alone with Virgil. She had failed to learn how Virgil made things grow. She spent hours helping him tend the plants. He realized she was trying to learn.

"Not so much water," he might say. Or, "Don't prune that branch. It's a healthy one. That blueberry bush'll die if you cut it."

Several times during a day she felt the urge to put her hand on his chest again but always resisted. After a week of this, she decided Virgil would have to go.

She told him one afternoon while Jason was still at school. Virgil was sitting on a bench he had made whittling on a piece of ornamental bamboo.

"Making a whistle for the boy," he said as she walked up.

She said, "I'm going to have to let you go. I'm sorry."

"I ain't had any more women in your office."

"I know. I appreciate that. But I'm going to have to let you go."

"Why?" he asked, making a deep cut in the bamboo.

"I can't afford you."

"You can't stay in business without me. Them plants'll die."

She looked at the plants, twice as many as when he started work and all of them healthy.

"I can do it," she said.

"You got your back up because it ain't you," he said in a soft, courteous voice.

She felt weak but managed to say, "I don't need you to run this place."

He placed one hand on her arm. Her body started to go limp. Suddenly she became angry, her body electric and alive, the skin on her legs and arms feeling prickly and beginning to itch.

"Don't touch me," she said, pushing his hand away. "Give me the key."

He hesitated a moment before placing it in her hand.

"Them new pear trees'll be dead in a week," he said.

She said, "Leave now. Don't come back."

"I'll go, but I'll be here. They could put me back in the penitentiary, but I'd still be here."

"I'll forget you the minute you leave."

"I won't forget."

"Get your things out of my office and get out."

She watched him walk out to the road and off her property, leaving the nursery filled with his plants, all green and healthy. Keeping them that way would not be easy without Virgil.

After supper that night, she decided to tell Jason.

"Virgil's gone," she said.

"Virg'll be back for me. I'm going with him," Jason said.

Jason began to click his tongue.

"Stop that!" she said, taking hold of both his arms and shaking him.

"I won't stay with you! I won't!" Jason screamed.

He tried to twist away. He was much stronger than she had expected, fighting silently like some kind of animal, biting and scratching until she had him on the floor, her knees over his arms.

"I want Virg!" he screamed up at her, the spit flying in her face.

"He's gone," she said, taking pleasure in telling him.

Jason began to cry, and she released him. He put his arms around her neck and hugged her.

"It's just us, now," she said.

She made him take a bath, which calmed him. Then she put him to bed and read stories to him until he went to sleep.

Something was wrong. She sat up in bed and realized the TV was not on, no sound of Saturday morning cartoons coming from the living room, Jason sitting charmed before the screen.

Jason was not in his bed, not in the bathroom, not out on the front porch. Gone to find Virgil, she thought. She dressed and drove slowly toward the nursery, looking for him on the sidewalk and then on the shoulder of the highway.

No one was at the nursery. She kept calling for Jason, but he did not answer. Then she was at the edge of the field. The grass was beginning to turn yellow at the top. Spiders had spun webs in the grass, and the webs glittered with tiny droplets of water.

"Jason, Jason," she called, receiving only the whine of the insects in reply.

She stepped into the field, wishing she had brought a hoe, but not wanting to take the time to go back for one. A few feet into the grass she found a narrow trail, worn by Jason's feet. She followed it, the tall grass closing in around her, in some places rising as tall as her head. The insects whined, and she expected at any moment to hear the buzz of a rattler. Spider webs blocked her path, single strands of silk across the trail, the webs sticky against her face. She walked slowly, taking only one or two steps at a time, keeping her eyes fixed on the ground for snakes. Then she heard the bamboo whistle, and the trail opened up into a cleared space beneath the sweet gum whose leaves were beginning to turn gold around the edges.

Jason and Virgil sat beneath the tree. Virgil wore a straw cowboy hat with a rattlesnake hatband.

"Jason, come here," she said.

Jason did not move.

"I was fixing to bring him home," Virgil said. "I was gone out of town. Had to come back. I got to know about you."

"Get off my property. Leave us alone," she said.

"You wanted to be with me ever since I came," Virgil said. "You knowed it, and I knowed it."

She wanted to reach out and touch him but stopped herself.

Virgil continued, "You want me."

"Go back to the car, Jason," she said.

"I want to stay with Virg," Jason said.

"Go on, boy," Virgil said.

Jason disappeared into the grass.

"Right here, right now. You wouldn't stop me," Virgil said.

"I will," she said.

He fixed his black eyes on her and took her arm, his fingers around her wrist. She tried to pull away, but he was too strong.

"You won't do nothing against me," Virgil said.

"I'll fight you," she said.

Virgil released her. She rubbed her wrist to rid it of the red marks left by his fingers.

"I killed a man over a woman like you," he said.

"I'm not like her," she said. "You couldn't do it again."

Virgil said, "No, not over a woman."

He stepped close again. She took his hand and placed it on her cheek, but he moved it to her hair, running his fingers through the short hair on the back of her neck.

"Like a fox's," he said.

She kissed him, but in that moment of giving way she pulled back, pushed him from her.

"You just can't make up your mind," he said. "I ain't got time to wait. A woman like you could be a year making up her mind. I'm going. Won't be back this time."

He turned and walked away, not taking the trail but going out through the other end of the field, the grass parting before him until he disappeared behind a clump of sumac, the leaves already turned red. From a tangle of blackberry bushes, a single insect gave a series of deep, halting clicks, refusing to concede the end of summer.

She wanted to run across the field after him but knew it was too late, that he was indeed gone.

"I don't have time for men," she said. "I've got a business to run."

Her voice sounded small in the emptiness of the field. She started to say it again but stopped and stood still, fixing her eyes on the sumac, the leaves still trembling from his passage.

LEMONFISH

My father is a labor organizer, a man workers like and trust the moment they set eyes on him. It's his gift. But it's been wasted in Mississippi where unions are not popular, a right-to-work law part of the state constitution. His one victory here was organizing the shipyard at Pascagoula. Then they cut back on building ships and laid off almost everyone.

After that the union had him going around trying to organize chicken plant workers and paper mill workers, but he didn't have all that much luck. The union was looking the situation over, waiting for an opportunity to present itself. They'd about given up on Mississippi.

In the fall, when I was still dating Sally Adams and came home from Ole Miss to take her to the Halloween dance, my mother told me he'd been out on the beach every day with his metal detector. Then around Christmas time—I was home again from the university—he found a gold doubloon. It's in the safe-deposit box at the bank. After Christmas he started taking night classes at the university extension to learn Spanish and scuba diving. He said I might be the first Garon to go to college, but he was a close second. Home again on spring break, I noticed the wall of his office was covered with maps of the coast, and the unpainted pine bookcases he'd knocked together were filled with books on Spanish history. He'd started talking about traveling to Madrid to research old Spanish shipping records.

Then he bought the pogy boat. Mother sends me a postcard once a week, written in that tiny hand of hers, the letters carefully printed. She can cram more information than you think anyone could onto a card. For the months of April and May the last sentence, written a little larger than the rest, was always the same: "It troubles me that Louis is working on the boat."

My father never mentioned the boat when we talked on the phone from time to time. I supposed that if he wanted to buy an old pogy boat and fix it up then that was his business. I guessed he was going to use it for treasure hunting. I liked that better than the other sidelines he had. There was something to do with trucks that wasn't quite legal. The coast has a Mafia of its own, and they're mixed up with the unions. I was glad I wasn't home, because I knew he'd have me sanding and painting.

In June I came home to start my summer job driving a forklift at a wholesale grocery warehouse. My car, needing a ring job I couldn't afford, barely made it to Biloxi. I'd had to add a quart of oil about every fifty miles, driving down out of the north Mississippi hills in a cloud of blue smoke. I'd brought my friend Jack, who's from Iowa, with me. He was going to try to get a job for the summer on a shrimp boat.

When we walk into the house, she and my father are sitting around watching a baseball game on TV, working their way through a couple of six packs of beer. My father, smelling of beer and cigarettes, throws his arms around me. Then Mother hugs me. They shake hands with Jack.

"Get Danny Glenn and Jack a beer," he says to Mother.

Mother goes off to the kitchen. I can smell gumbo cooking. It's got okra in it, so to please me she's left out the filé to keep the okra from turning slimy. I can't stand slimy okra.

"We'll go out on the boat Saturday," he says. "You boys can do some fishing."

He starts telling us how he'd fixed up the boat: rebuilt the engines, installed a plywood canopy aft of the pilothouse, put in a live bait well.

Mother has come back into the room with the beers. As I look over my father's shoulder, she rolls her eyes.

"What are you going to do with it if they send you to Kansas?" she asks.

He ignores her. She sits down and begins to file her nails. She always does that when she's mad.

"I got a couple of hunches about where that ship went down," he says. "I find anything, investors will want to come in. I know some people with money."

He has this theory that a ship from the annual Spanish treasure fleet, blown halfway across the Gulf by a hurricane, had sunk off one of the barrier islands. There's a chain of them about twenty miles off the coast: Ship Island, Cat Island, Petit Bois, which we pronounce Petty Boy. Not like they teach you in French class.

I try to imagine him not working for the union but can't. He's a man with big forearms, a thick chest, and huge hands. He can palm a basketball

with no trouble at all. Yet he can use those same big fingers to roll a cigarette with one hand. He'd worked in the steel mills in Birmingham when
he was a young man. I like to imagine him shaping the white hot metal
right in the mouth of the furnace, moving casually but expertly with sparks
flying about him. In the summer and spring he wears a white polyester
sport coat and in the colder months a dark suit. They are cheap, ill-fitting
clothes, but he has a way of making them look good, especially after they're
rumpled and covered with cigarette ashes. I wouldn't want him sitting
across the negotiating table from me at three in the morning.

We have dinner: gumbo, cornbread, raw oysters, and rice. I show Jack
how to open the shells with an oyster knife and how to eat them by putting
the open shell to your lips and sucking them off it, that taste of oyster and
sea water in your mouth. Mother does the dishes while we watch the baseball game and drink. Then the game is over, and Mother goes off to bed
and then Jack. My father and I watch the late news.

"I got you a good deal on a new car," he says.

"I can't afford it," I say.

I'd barely made it through the last month of school. I needed all the
money I'd make in the summer. And I knew that the check my parents sent
me every month might not be there if my father decided to quit the union.
That's what Mother was worried about.

"It's a trade," he says. "You be on the Pass Christian Bridge tomorrow
at twelve o'clock."

I decide not to argue. Someone owed him a favor or wanted to ask him
a favor. And it didn't seem likely that I'd lose on the deal.

"Sure," I say. "I'll be there."

Then he had me tell him about what I'd done in school that semester.
I'd taken an anthropology course, and he was concerned that it might have
shaken my belief in God.

"I go to mass every week," I say.

"I don't," he says. "Can't spare the time. Father Braud has been asking
about me. I've been busy with the boat."

We sit and talk like this until after midnight.

Jack and I are on the Pass Christian Bridge at noon. This guy pulls up
behind us in a white Chevrolet convertible that looks like it's just come out
of a clean-up shop. I'm glad there's a stiff breeze blowing so he won't notice
the smoke from my car's exhaust. The gulls sail around, riding the wind,
swooping up above the bridge like white pieces of paper.

"You Danny Glenn Garon?" he asks.

He's wearing a pair of mechanic's overalls with Bobby stitched in red thread over his left breast pocket.

"That's me," I say.

And then, although I can't quite believe it, he hands me the keys. We exchange papers; he gets in my car and drives off. Jack and I are left standing looking at the almost new car, the engine running so smooth we can barely hear it. I'm thinking that I can sell it and buy something cheaper. Use the money for my junior year abroad in Germany. I'm an international business major. There's a scholarship I'm after, but I can't count on winning that.

"What's going on?" Jack asks.

"It's probably hot," I say.

I look at the papers. No bank owns the car. I've never heard of the name on the papers.

"Well, if it is, you didn't steal it," Jack says.

I know I can't go back to my father and tell him I don't want the car because I think it's stolen. I wonder what favor this repays, a favor my father might need soon if things don't work out for him. I promise myself to take very good care of the car so it can be resold easily.

The pogy boat sits there among the sailboats and cabin cruisers at the marina, looking like a deformed child among a group of perfect children. He's put a peak on the plywood canopy like a house roof.

Noah's Ark, I think.

"Man, we can sit in the shade and drink beer and fish," Jack says.

Being from Iowa, there's no way he can know anything about boats. My father has got him a lead on a shrimp boat job so he is feeling good.

We go out of the harbor too fast, our wake causing those fancy boats to rock against each other. A few people yell at my father, but he ignores them. Most of those boats belong to what he calls "the enemy." It's like he assumes that every one of them is the property of a factory manager. That's what I'm going to college to learn to be, one of "them." And I wonder if he's ever considered that.

The Gulf is blue and calm, like a big lake. The sailboats from the yacht club are just kind of drifting about, girls lying face down on the teak decks with their bikini tops unbuttoned.

We rig up our rods and troll for sea trout. The old man insists on running the boat, but he goes much too fast. Pretty soon our lines are all twisted and tangled. When I complain, he says he's decided to go to Ship Island. We can fish on the way back.

Jack and I sit on the lawn chairs under the canopy and drink beer. Then we go up and watch a porpoise play in the bow wake. We pass another sailboat, girls lying out on the deck, basking in the sun like lizards.

We yell at them and they wave back. The boys don't wave. They laugh and motion to one another to look at my father's strange creation.

Back under the canopy, I sit and think of first time I really understood what my father's job was like.

We are driving in the car, the seats filled with mimeographed flyers and old newspapers. I smell the blue ink of the mimeograph. I remember hearing the clack of the machine as my father and his friends turned out the flyers. But now we're alone.

There is a plant, a huge building with rows of lighted windows. I close my eyes and see a fence and a crowd of men milling about. He gives me a stack of flyers and sends me out into the crowd. There's a smell to the men I can't identify, that effluvium of sweat and tobacco and something else which could be coal dust or cotton lint or acid from a paper mill.

I work the crowd, the big hands reaching down to take the flyers. Then there's a whistle and sirens and men are shouting. I'm snatched up by a stranger, a huge man, and we're running. There're a series of popping sounds like firecrackers going off. The asphalt changes to gravel and then to grass. I'm lifted over a fence.

A car appears before my eyes, the door opening and my father beckoning me. The man throws me on the front seat and gets in after me, slamming the door behind him. I dive over the back seat. My father drives fast down the road, both men cursing long and eloquently as I lie on the stacks of paper.

Then they have exhausted themselves and are silent. I listen to the hiss of the tires on the road. My father turns in his seat, a smile on his face.

"You, Danny Glenn," he says. "You're my boy."

The big man reaches back and lifts me into the front seat where I sit beside them, as we drive down the road that runs between ploughed fields of red earth.

A small fishing boat crosses our bow, then circles us, the men waving. The old man slows down, and they come alongside.

"Got any ice to spare?" one of the men asks.

They're weekend fishermen, a little overweight from their office jobs, their necks and arms burned red from the sun.

"We've come all the way from Chandeleur Sound," the driver says. "We got lemonfish. We're out of ice. They'll spoil in this heat."

So my father gives them all our ice, and that's the end of any serious fishing for us. That's Louis Garon all right. He'd give anyone the coat off his back if they asked.

We end up at Ship Island. Jack's never been there. While my father plays the slot machines, probably his real reason for coming all the way out to federal property where it's legal, we wander about in Fort Massachusetts. The sea has taken part of it, toppling the red bricks into the water. One of these days a hurricane will come along and sweep it all away.

Then we go down to the beach where airmen from Keesler, who've come out on one of the excursion boats, have stripped down to their underwear and are swimming in the surf. We join them and then sit on the beach, letting the sun and the strong breeze that's come up dry us off.

My father is ahead at the slot machines, but I can't persuade him to leave. He's drinking whiskey now, a styrofoam cup full of it on one side of the machine he's selected and a cup of tokens on the other.

"You can play too," he says.

"No, thanks," I say.

I think of those identical sentences on Mother's postcards. She's right. The boat was a bad idea. He needs to get back to work. I'd feel better if he were getting threatening phone calls at two in the morning and if all night meetings were being held in our kitchen. Jack and I return to the boat and drink beer.

"You'll fix me up?" Jack asks. "You know some girls?"

I say I will and I think of those girls lying on the deck of the sailboat. Once I become the "enemy" I might have one of those boats and know girls like that. They're the same girls who date the fraternity boys at school. I'm majoring in international business because I'm good at languages and I want to travel. So far I've hardly been out of Mississippi. I suspect my father would like to have me go to law school and became a union lawyer. He's hinted at that before. Certainly he couldn't be happy about me going to work for some *Fortune* 500 company.

About mid-afternoon my father wanders back to the boat. He's won two hundred dollars which he says he's going to put into navigational gear for the boat. We start back, the Gulf still calm.

He calls me up to the pilot house. Now he's got charts spread out.

"Danny Glenn, we're going to take a look," he says.

He glances back toward Jack.

●

"We'll just say we're diving for fun," he says.

"At what?" I ask.

I think I already know the answer and knowing makes me uneasy.

"The ship," he says. "The *Cuervo*."

That's Spanish for "raven."

"I've got full air tanks, everything we need," he says.

I don't like the idea. None of us should be diving after drinking all day.

"We can take a look at the spot," I say. "We don't have to dive."

"We'll see," he says.

It takes us a couple of hours to locate the place. We drop anchor off Petit Bois in fifteen feet of water. The palms and pines of the island look cool and inviting, but this time of year it's not a good place to be, a paradise for bugs and snakes. There's a shrimp boat working about a mile away, the booms that support its nets spread out like a pair of wings.

He puts on his scuba gear without any further discussion about whether we should dive. So I get into mine because I don't want him going down alone. He tells Jack we're going to spearfish.

The visibility is good below, the afternoon sunlight shooting down through the clear water. The sand is white, the bottom bare and desert-like. I watch a torpedo-shaped barracuda go shooting off. We swim slowly about. Every now and then he probes the bottom with the tip of his spear, stirring up little clouds of sand.

I wonder what's going through his mind as we swim almost weightless amid the bubbles from our regulators. I keep careful track of how long we're down. At twenty minutes I tap him on the shoulder and point up. He pauses for a moment and then shakes his head in agreement.

Jack is disappointed that we've speared no fish. We stow the gear away and then start back. My father and I sit in the lawn chairs and talk while Jack has the wheel, steering the course my father has given him.

"It's down there," he says. "All I need to do is find a bar of silver or a few doubloons. Then the investors will come in."

Like swapping cars on the bridge, I think.

He talks on and on about the sunken ship. He knows her tonnage and her construction, the manifest listing the cargo, and the name of her captain. It seems unlikely, almost impossible to me, that the hurricane could have driven them here on their way from Panama to Havana, loaded with gold and silver from the mines of Peru. But he's got it figured out. His excitement frightens me. I see him standing in line at the welfare office. I see Mother handing the clerk food stamps at the grocery store.

Then the engine quits. We suppose that Jack in his inexperience has done something. But we can't get it started again.

We open the hatch and look at the engine. No one has any idea what's wrong. After we've exhausted the obvious things: gas, clogged fuel line, battery, I try over and over to start it. But it just coughs and sputters. Nothing.

My father calls the marina on the radio for a tow. We throw out the anchor, although the Gulf is so calm we don't really need it. Then we sit and wait. Jack goes to sleep, the boat rocking gently in the swells.

"I may just put in a new engine," he says. "I come out here in rough weather and I'll need something dependable."

I wish he would find a ship full of gold and silver, but I know he won't. Treasure hunting is going to break his heart.

"Are they sending you to Kansas?" I ask.

"I don't know," he says. "They've been sending me places for twenty years. They say go and I go."

I know we're just going to talk around it, and after all it's none of my business. No matter what he chooses to do, nothing will change that much for me. He's taught me to take care of myself. I imagine us spending the night out here, the sun dropping down into the water and the stars coming out, bright and brilliant in the sky. Way off, we'd see the glow from the mainland. There in the darkness, while Jack slept, we'd quietly talk, and by morning we'd understand each other.

"Let's get in the water," he says.

We go over the side, the water deep and cool. He's been drinking too much beer, his stomach turned flabby, his paunch bigger than I remember. He floats on his back, a trick I've never mastered.

"How deep do you think it is?" he asks.

"Twenty, thirty feet," I say.

The Gulf is very shallow. You can walk out from the beach for a quarter of a mile sometimes before the water rises above your waist and you reach the channel.

He makes a graceful surface dive, and I'm left alone to listen to the swells slapping against the hull. I think of that day I was separated from him, the big man's arms snatching me up. He has been down a long time, but then I haven't timed him, so I have no real way of knowing. I start to count. By the time I reach fifteen, he breaks water beside me.

"Look!" he says. "Look!"

He's grinning at me, his voice excited.

"What?" I ask, playing along.

He opens his hand and there's a small conch in it.

"It could be another doubloon," he says. "One day that's what it's gonna be."

"You take that car," I say.

He laughs.

"I can't go driving that into places," he says. "If you were cleaning chickens for a living, would you trust a man who drives a car like that?"

I've never known him to buy a new car.

"I guess not," I say.

"Don't you go selling that car," he says. "Mr. John Lefleur won't like you doing that. Last time I had lunch with him he asked me what I wanted. I said, 'Nothing.' He just laughed and said he'd seen you driving that old car, burning more oil than gas. Said you were going to get arrested for pollution."

He laughs at the joke made by the man who runs most of the prostitution and gambling on the coast, but I don't. I think of saying that I'm going to get arrested for driving a hot car, but instead I say nothing.

"He wanted to trade. I couldn't say no."

We circle each other, treading water, and I want to take hold of him, fearful he'll dive again, fearful that the net he's woven for himself will in the end catch me up too. I want to feel him wet and slippery in my arms but at the same time solid and warm. My father.

He floats on his back again, placing the conch shell on his chest. The inside is pink, the folds spiraling around to where the animal is hiding.

"I won the price of the tow," he said. "Your old man is lucky."

"Sure," I say.

He hears something in my voice. He flips over, the conch disappearing into the water, and starts treading water again. He looks hard at me.

"You think I'm a fool?" he asks.

"No, sir," I say.

And I realize that I don't want to discuss this with him. It was a mistake thinking I wanted to.

"This country could be a worker's paradise," he says. "That's what I thought. That's what I still think. Those guys who run the factories, they want it all. Sure I've had to sleep with John Lefleur, but he's no worse than the legislature or the owners. Sometimes he can get things done."

"But you want to quit," I say.

"I'm tired. Every man's got a right to get tired."

"So I should go to law school? Become a union lawyer?"

"I never said you should do that."

He's beginning to breathe a little heavier, and I know I should suggest that we swim back to the boat. But I don't. I guess I like it that his body is failing ever so slightly while I could stay out here and tread water all day.

"You didn't have to say it," I say.

"You do what you want," he says. "Just find something worth doing. Something important."

"Like treasure hunting?"

He laughs and pushes back his thinning hair with one hand from where it's fallen into his face. I can see the crescent shaped scar on his skull, left there from a battle at a plant entrance. When I was a kid, I liked to run my fingers over it. It was just as good as the wounds other kids' fathers brought home from Korea.

"Yeah, I think I'm going to become a treasure hunter," he says.

"What about mother?" I ask.

"I can take early retirement. We'll get by."

"It won't be enough."

I think about what will happen if I don't get the scholarship to go to Germany, how tough it's going to be to come up with the money. I'll have to find a better part-time job at school.

"Don't you sell that car," he says. "Just remember that I can get you that union scholarship to law school."

So there it is, I think.

It's not that quitting the union and his treasure hunting is some elaborate ploy to get me committed to four years of union work after they've paid for law school. But I know it's been in the back of his mind all along.

"I don't think so," I say.

He laughs.

"You can do whatever you want," he says. "Just be careful with that car. Take good care of it."

I want the car to be the same as those tokens that came pouring out of the slot machine. Something totally free and unsullied, with no strings attached. Just like those doubloons he's after, incorruptible, lying shining on the white sand. I fear for what might happen to him if he devotes himself to searching for treasure, and I fear what will happen if he keeps working for the union. If he stays he'll have a job, but he'll have to deal with men like John Lefleur and workers who're convinced that paternalism is best.

"Come on, Danny Glenn," he says, his voice strong. "We stay out here too long and we'll be bait for sharks."

We swim for the boat. And I'm glad. The next thing you know he'll be telling me there're bars of Spanish gold below us, spilling out of the broken ribs of a galleon. I imagine us diving together down into some fabulously deep crease in the belly of the ocean, past the sunlight into cold darkness, the pressure enormous. I see the wreck, lying with its bow thrust up at an angle, our lights playing over it. And he swims ahead and pauses at a gash in its side. He enters, motioning for me to follow, and I do, although I fear that among the rotted rigging and shattered spars lies not gold but an intricate darkness from which we'll not escape.

OPENING DAY

Anita watched Lenore amble across the lawn and was struck again by the duckfooted, careless, but at the same time light sort of way she had of walking. Once Anita's husband told her how he'd persuaded Lenore to practice walking a lane line of the high school track in an attempt to teach her to set her feet down straight. Anita imagined Lenore navigating the white line like a tightrope walker and probably doing it too slowly to suit Fisher, who was always impatient.

It was ballet that ruined Lenore's feet, Fisher told Anita, all those ballet lessons his ex-wife took in Memphis. But walking the track didn't do any good. In a few days she was back to her old way. Fisher had said it wasn't changing the way she walked that was so important, but he'd hoped if he could change one thing, more important things might follow. In the case of Lenore it didn't work. As far as Anita could tell the only good ballet did was make her graceful. Now it was like she was floating across the lawn.

As Anita stood in the doorway and watched Lenore, the sweet scent of a haunch of venison Fisher had just placed in the smoker drifted through the house, food for friends he'd invited to shoot doves on his field. Lenore had brought their son Jeff down from Memphis for the hunt.

A month into their marriage, Fisher had received a cash settlement from Lenore. Fisher and Anita began spending it on cocaine, the money slipping away from them, the balance in the checkbook shrinking faster than she'd thought possible. There were dimly remembered weekends in Memphis and New Orleans where she drifted through a tangled web of parties, the frantic beat of the music carrying her along, and now the voices of the people lingered in her memory like the mad chorus of insects that nightly buzzed and clicked and trilled from the cypress brake behind the house. She remembered Fisher swimming the river at New Orleans to win a bet, his body glistening with grease he'd applied against the cold water, and she not thinking for a moment he might drown. She had never thought they had been driven just by their desire for cocaine. The drug was only the catalyst that awakened some deeper, more subtle force. It was as if that Delta boom or bust prodigality of their ancestors, tied for generations to the rise and fall of the price of cotton, had suddenly been unleashed.

They told each other their life was a normal one. Fisher boasted he could farm just fine while high; Anita more cautiously claimed that she was still a good teacher. Until the day her mind got changed. She was teaching a history lesson to her sixth-grade class and at the same time thinking of Fisher's hands on her. The children were already distracted by a crop duster working the field outside her classroom window. She thought of pressing herself against Fisher, closing herself around his thickness, the very shape of her body seeming to change, to flow, and then amazingly she was with him and in the classroom at the same time and she felt his body and heard herself mouthing the words about the Mississippi statesman L. Q. C. Lamar and Fisher was taking them both further and further away from Mississippi history. Then Sammy Percy was making a sucking noise like a fish, and the children were laughing. She wondered what they saw; she felt naked and exposed. She wanted the image of her and Fisher entwined together to go away; she wanted to reclaim the shape of herself. But it was only with a struggle that she pushed the dream of love out of her mind. A ripple of laughter ran through the classroom.

"That crop duster is going to hit a wire," she said.

It was such a relief to her to look at the plane as it hung absurdly suspended a few feet above the field. It looked to her like a toy and not a real plane at all with a man inside who was facing the obstacle of the wires. Knowing that he was going to be able to do it made her feel safe.

Caught by her ploy, the children swiveled in their seats to watch as the pilot banked the plane over the telephone wires, the sound of the straining engine reaching them a moment later. By then Anita had composed herself.

The next day Anita wrote a check for a pecan grove, where they'd already talked of building a new house, and gave the builder an advance, and all of Lenore's settlement money was gone.

Lenore wandered across the yard, like a deer browsing, stopping every now and then to look up into the big oaks and pecans as if something had been revealed to her up in those branches that had been denied to the rest of the world. Lenore's fine blond hair swirled about her face as she stopped and looked back at her grandmother's house, Miss Louise dead two years. The old woman had raised her, paid for the private school in Memphis and the ballet lessons. The house Lenore had claimed she was going to restore was falling down. If the hole in the roof wasn't fixed, the house would be gone by this time next year. Lenore claimed she was sick, that she had Epstein-Barr. But Anita was not so sure. Fisher had warned Anita that Lenore could be tricky. She could be dangerous.

"Where's Jeffery?" Lenore asked.

She stood in front of Anita now, looking over her shoulder at the inside of house which had been built for the farm manager. Anita hated the house with its furniture upholstered in plastic and a pool table in the dining room. If she'd started the new house project earlier, she reflected, the pool table would be where it belonged. The house would be in order. Now the fight to overcome Fisher's inertia was just not worth it. Whenever Anita despaired about the way they were living, she found solace by imagining the new white house with its wide porch among the rows of green trees.

Fisher's hand was on her shoulder. He had come silently up behind her.

"Playing with that dog," Fisher said. "Sleeps with that dog, eats with it. Why don't you let him take it back to Memphis with you?"

Lenore laughed and shook her head, throwing out her shining halo of blond hair. Anita had to admit that she envied Lenore her hair.

Anita knew that Jeff and the gun-shy pup were under the pool table. Fisher knew it too.

"Where?" Lenore asked.

"Beats me," Fisher said.

"He's too young to be driving a tractor," Lenore said. "I wish you wouldn't let him."

Jeff had spent the morning cutting the grass with a small tractor that had a mower attached. Now Miss Louise's lawn of three acres had a park-like look to it again.

A series of whoops and cheers came from the house. The football game on TV had finally started.

"I'm teaching him the things he needs to know," Fisher said.

Anita considered how Fisher treated Lenore and decided it was unhealthy. She wondered if "unhealthy" was the right word and decided it was. There was something pathological in his treatment of Lenore.

"Just like you had that dog trained to be gun shy," she said.

Fisher had been trying to get his money back from the trainer.

Fisher put his hand on Anita's arm. Suddenly her feeling of certainty about their life in the new house vanished, and she found herself wondering if things were going to be different when they moved there. But even in this house, no better than a cabin at a deer camp, Fisher had been sweet to her. She thought of waking up on Sunday mornings and smelling the coffee he'd made or opening some present he'd bought her in Memphis. She wondered if five years from now, ten years from now, that would be enough.

"He'll kill his first buck this year," Fisher said. "You'll see."

"Jeffery," Lenore called out, but her voice was lost in the noise of the football game.

"I bought that dog for Jeff," Fisher said.

"Jeffery," Lenore said. "Jeff sounds like a name you'd give to a horse. And you bought it for yourself. Once something is not perfect you don't want it anymore. You're going to have a hard time growing old."

Anita looked closely at Lenore. The disease—if it was really true—instead of making her tired and lazy-like had given her a strange fevered energy.

"OK, we'll call him Jeffery," Anita said.

Lenore didn't bother to answer but walked past them like a queen into the living room. The football fans, her friends too, acknowledged her presence with waves and nods before returning their attention to the game. Ole Miss and Memphis State.

"I wish you wouldn't fight with her," Anita said to Fisher.

"We'll be in the new house before Christmas," Fisher said. "Then when she comes here she won't bother anybody but the squirrels." He sighed. "Crazy Lenore."

Anita and Fisher went back inside. Lenore found Jeff beneath the table with the dog and crawled under it to talk with him. Anita considered how childlike Lenore was and wondered why Fisher was ever interested in her. But, she reflected, Lenore was sweet to the boy. Lenore would make a good teacher. Anita could imagine the children gazing spellbound at Lenore's shining hair, at those fluttering white hands. But then she decided that Lenore would never last. The children would sense her instability, and one day in their casual mindless cruelty, they'd push her over the edge.

Lenore crawled out from under the table and, ignoring the game, walked up to Anita.

"We need to talk," Lenore said.

Anita followed her outside.

"You know he wanted to shoot both of us," Lenore said.

Anita had heard the story before from Fisher. Now she was going to be treated to Lenore's version.

Instead of facing her, Lenore was looking toward Miss Louise's house. In the settlement Lenore and Fisher divided Lenore's grandmother's farm of ten thousand acres down the middle. The house was hers. Fisher got the gin. Fisher liked to say that he paid for the gin with his finger. For ten years he ran the gin and escaped with only the loss of the tip of his index finger, a good record for a ginman who had to work amid unprotected belts and gears. Fisher wasn't like Lenore's people. His father made his living cutting pulpwood. His mother died when he was three. But Fisher had pulled himself out of that miserable life and worked his way through the state agricultural university.

"Fisher said you were both drunk," Anita said.

She said this because it didn't appear as if Lenore was going to say anything more. Anita felt tired, like she hadn't been to sleep for a couple of days. Fisher had warned her how Lenore drained the energy from a person.

"That's right, we were drunk," Lenore said. "Jeffery saved me. You remember that. You have some children quick so you'll be safe from Fisher."

Anita started to speak, but Lenore held up her hand for silence.

"Neither of us could remember exactly what the fight was about afterwards because we were very drunk," Lenore said. "It doesn't matter. Probably his awful family. Fisher worries about that. I never cared. I do know that he went to the bedroom and came back with that pistol he kept in a holster slung over the bedpost. Does he have one hung over yours?"

Anita decided not to respond. She wanted to hear the rest of it, not get involved in a discussion of her marriage with Fisher.

"I ran to the bedroom and woke Jeffery," Lenore said. "He was only four. Then I sat in the rocking chair and told Fisher to shoot Jeffery first."

Anita remembered Fisher telling her the story. "Just think about that," Fisher had said. "She wanted me to shoot the boy first. If that's not the sign of a hard-hearted woman, I don't know what is."

And now Anita tried to imagine how it must have been, the child's eyes dull with sleep, his blond hair rumpled, his head thrown back against Lenore's heaving breasts.

"Don't you see," Lenore said. "You'll end up having to do something like that. Living with Fisher makes you—" She searched a moment for the word. "Desperate."

Then she shook her hair, running her hands through it, and walked back across the huge yard toward the decaying house.

Anita thought there was the possibility of change; she told herself to be patient. Much of the problem was Lenore's fault. After all, Lenore had lived with him for ten years and had managed to make not even the simplest civilizing improvements. Anita liked the idea of changing Fisher. Then she realized that was the definition of her love for him: a looking forward to change. She pictured them having a party in the new house, the circular driveway filled with substantial cars, the college boys, hired by the Memphis caterer, carrying trays of drinks among the crowd that had spilled out onto the porch. Once they moved into the house everything would change.

They shot in a sunflower field, the big heads drooping on the ends of their stalks. It'd been a dry summer. A field hand had bush-hogged the field, leaving a few rows standing to provide cover for the shooters. It was hot, but Anita liked the heat. She'd met Fisher at the end of August three years ago when they were both running the Delta 10k in Greenville.

Anita and Fisher took a stand in the shade from a cypress brake that ran the length of the field. Fisher was worried about Mike, his lab, getting over-heated. Anita was dressed in khaki hunting clothes she'd ordered from a catalog, while Fisher wore a pith helmet, jeans, and a dark green silk shirt. Jeff with his .410 was about thirty yards to their left. Jeff had shot two doves; Anita had downed five. She was not particularly interested in hunting. Today, she thought, would be a good day for a race. Most racers couldn't tolerate the heat as well as she.

Fisher already had shot fifty doves, thirty-five over the limit. Anita had argued with him about it, but Fisher was set on killing a hundred doves.

"I don't care about any limit," Fisher had said. "Like my old man always said, those limits are to keep ordinary folks in line so rich folks'll be able to shoot all the birds they want. Now I guess I'm one of those rich folks, at least as long as the bank don't call in my loans."

Anita thought about Lenore's warning.

Jeff brought down his third dove.

"That's it, boy," Fisher yelled.

As Mike started to bolt after the bird, Fisher commanded him to stay. The dog whined in disappointment. Jeff retrieved the bird and held it up to show them.

Lenore's red truck entered the field.

"Damn," Fisher said. "I'd rather it was the game warden. I can never understand why she drives a truck. She knows nothing about farming. Why to her it's like cotton and beans come out out of the ground by magic."

Lenore stopped at each of the stands. She collected the birds and chat-
ted with her friends. Anita imagined Lenore doing this during each of the
ten years she and Fisher were married. Lenore didn't like to shoot. Another
one of Lenore's mistakes.

"Why can't she stay in Memphis?" Fisher asked. "I told her I'd come
pick him up."

Anita looked at Jeff, who had just shot three times at a high-flying dove
and missed.

"He can't hear," Fisher said.

"It's not good for us to get in the habit of talking about her around Jeff,"
Anita said.

Doves flew toward them, the birds twisting in the air, their sharp-edged
wings moving steadily. The others shot at them. Two, then three dropped.
The birds darted around the side of a big cypress and vanished into the brake.

"Just look at her," Fisher said. "Did you lock up the house?"

"Yes," Anita said.

All morning Lenore had been asking Fisher if they were going to lock the
house. Anita imagined she'd asked Fisher the same question a dozen times.

"I don't want Lenore laying her hands on our things," Fisher said.

"Don't you get her stirred up," Anita said.

She imagined Lenore in their bedroom, sifting through the contents of
their dresser.

"Bird, up!" Jeff yelled.

Anita turned and swung from left to right, her most difficult shot. She
brought the bird down. Mike looked up at her, waiting for the command
to fetch. She gave it, and the dog ran off across the field.

"Have you noticed how Lenore smiles?" Fisher asked. "Thinks she's a
movie star. All those white teeth. Capped, every one of them. She likes to
deceive folks."

The truck came bouncing across the furrows. Jeff ran up to his mother
and showed her his doves. Lenore smiled at them. Lenore's teeth didn't
look capped to her.

"I need the key to the house," Lenore said.

Fisher drew in his breath sharply.

"You can put 'em in Miss Louise's house," Fisher said.

Anita didn't want a fight to start. She didn't want Lenore to ruin the day.

"The refrigerator is broken," Lenore said. "They'll spoil in this heat."

"You could take'em to Sam's," Fisher said.

Sam, the gin foreman, lived nearby.

"Why would I want to do that?" Lenore asked.

"That doesn't make any sense at all," Anita said.

She stepped forward and handed Lenore her own set of keys.

Then they loaded the doves into Nieman-Marcus shopping bags and set the bags behind the front seat of the truck. There were already four full bags hidden there.

"Don't you get caught by the game warden," Fisher cautioned.

Lenore laughed.

"I'm not worried about Billy Smart," she said. "Remember, I went to high school with him."

Anita imagined Lenore talking herself out of a ticket, the warden fascinated by the way her hands moved and the glitter of her green eyes.

"I wouldn't count on it," Fisher said. "People do change."

Lenore laughed and put the truck in gear.

"Some never change at all," she said.

She drove off fast, the truck bouncing over the rough ground.

Anita looked at Fisher to see how he reacted, but he was already scanning the sky for more birds.

Jeff finally got his limit of fifteen birds, just before he ran out of shells. Anita watched as he lined the birds up on the ground and counted them. Then he carefully put them one by one back into his game bag.

"Shoot yourself a few more," Fisher said.

"No, sir," Jeff said. "This is enough for me."

Anita wondered if Lenore had instructed him to stop when he reached the limit. Or maybe he decided on his own, the same way she decided she no longer should teach school while high on cocaine.

"These are our doves," Fisher said. "I could've sold these sunflowers or planted this field in beans or cotton."

"I've got enough," Jeff said.

"You shoot until you're out of shells," Fisher said.

"If he wants to quit, let him quit," Anita said. "He's probably tired. I'm tired too. We'll get us a cold drink."

Anita started to walk off with Jeff toward the truck parked on the edge of the brake.

"There's no reason to be quitting," Fisher said. "He's got shells left."

"You should stop too," Anita said.

"Dammit, this boy has already been ruined living with a woman," Fisher said.

Jeff was watching a dragonfly that had lit on the end of his gun barrel. Its wings, glistening as if they had been shellacked, were a bluish color.

"I'll shoot some more," Jeff said. "I don't mind."

He began pushing shells into the magazine of the automatic shotgun.

"I mind," Anita said. "Fisher, I want you to take me home."

"You'd want him up in Memphis too, learning the wrong things," Fisher said. "That boy'll be running this place one day. He's got to learn."

"Learn what?" Anita asked.

"How things are," Fisher said. "Those that take things get them."

"Oh, that's an original thought," Anita said.

Jeff shot.

Anita looked up and saw a dove go sailing with fixed wings over their heads and into the brake. A few grey and white feathers came floating down amid the swarms of hovering dragonflies.

Mike whined. He wanted the bird.

"Hunt dead," Fisher said, motioning toward the brake.

"No, wait," Anita said.

She made a grab for Mike's collar but missed. Mike ran off and disappeared into the brake through a head-high jungle of weeds and briars.

"You look for wounded game," Fisher said to Jeff.

Jeff had a serious expression on his face, his lips pressed tightly together.

"Yes, sir," Jeff said. "I know."

"Knowing and doing are two different things," Fisher said.

"Call him out," Anita said.

They heard the dog casting about in the thick cover.

"He'll find your bird," Fisher said.

A yelp came from the brake. Mike crashed about in briars for a few moments and broke free, coming toward them on a dead run. Anita knew what had happened. It made her sick to think of it.

"I told you," Anita said.

Mike ran into Fisher's arms. The dog whined and shook his head.

Fisher ran his hands over the side of Mike's head, the dog trembling under his touch. A spot just under his left eye was already starting to swell.

"Damn you," Anita said. "That brake is full of moccasins. But you didn't care. You knew—"

Mike was suddenly having trouble breathing. Fisher wrapped his arms about him. Jeff began to cry. The vet was thirty miles away.

"Hang on," Anita said. "Hang on."

Anita didn't know why she was saying it. The words sounded like they were being spoken by someone else.

Mike sank to the soft ploughed earth. Now his breath was coming in gasps, his mud-caked sides heaving. Then he stopped breathing, that frantic rise and fall still. Anita thought it was too sudden to be believed, as if the dog were no more substantial than an air-filled paper bag that had been casually crushed.

"Do something," Anita said.

"God, he's dead," Fisher said solemnly.

Anita knelt over the dog and pulled open his jaws. She put her mouth over his, dog slobber covering her face. Surprisingly it had a sweet taste. She breathed in and, taking another breath, breathed again. Over and over. After ten minutes of this she was exhausted, and the dog was still not breathing.

"He's gone," Jeff said. The boy's voice quavered but then was strong. "You tried."

Jeff placed his hand on her back, moving it gently in a small circle. Anita put her ear to the dog's side. There was no heartbeat. The smell of the brake—a mixture of dead cypress leaves, cotton defoliant, and mud—rose out of the dog's damp coat. Anita felt like crying, but she was too exhausted. Fisher was crying. Yet his face appeared to her as flat and one-dimensional as if it had been cut out of a piece of the gin's tin roof. Jeff was crying too.

"We'll take him over to Sam's later," Fisher said. "Sam'll bury him."

They wrapped Mike in a tarp and put the dog in the back of the truck.

"Damn you, damn you, damn you," Anita said.

The words rushed out of her. Fisher just stood there and gaped stupidly. She tried to imagine him holding her in his arms but she couldn't. It was as if he were some strange hunter who had wandered uninvited into the field.

"Go on back to the house," Fisher said.

Anita started for the truck.

"May I go too?" the boy asked.

Fisher looked down on his son's tear-wet face.

"You don't want to stay and hunt?"

"No, sir."

"Go stay with the women then."

The boy got in the truck beside Anita.

"After a while you send Lenore or Sam for our birds," Fisher said.

Anita looked away from him and drove out of the field.

They buried the dog in the backyard of Miss Louise's house, a spot Lenore chose beneath a big pecan. The women took turns with a pick. The black earth had been split and baked hard by the heat, the handle of the pick vibrating uncomfortably in Anita's hands as she swung it, but after they'd gone down a foot the digging got easier. Jeff shoveled out the dirt. Although the field was too far away, Anita imagined that she could hear the shooting. No one cried over the dog anymore.

Then Lenore made them iced tea in a crystal pitcher. They sent Jeff to Anita's house for ice. Anita imagined Miss Louise selecting the pitcher in a Memphis shop, her hands, that were too big for such a tiny woman, moving carefully over it. Then Anita imagined the pitcher sitting in the center of the big dining room table, the mahogany now gone crazy. They all sat on the porch of Miss Louise's house and drank. Jeff soon went off to let his dog out of the pen. They watched him tossing a frisbee to the pup out beneath the big trees.

"I'm sorry I came," Lenore said.

"It's your house," Anita said. "You've a right to come here."

They sat together and Anita thought she was going to say something to Lenore about Miss Louise's crystal pitcher, but instead, to her surprise, she began telling Lenore about running a race in Arizona, how her sweat evaporated like magic in the low humidity, such a change from Mississippi. And Lenore told Anita about dancing in the Tennessee mountains, how in the summer they danced at an old CCC camp, how her body soared off the hand-planed oak boards. Anita made another pitcher of tea. Jeff came by the porch from time to time but then went into the house to watch TV.

"Do you think you'll stay married to Fisher?" Lenore asked.

Anita didn't reply at once but sat there thinking. The sun was beginning to set over the levee and the line of trees which marked the river. This was the first mention either of them had made of Fisher all afternoon. Anita imagined Fisher staying on in the field to hunt the birds as they came in to roost in the brake. She pictured fire uncoiling from the barrel of his gun.

"I don't know," Anita said. "Maybe not."

To her surpise Anita found that the words were easy to say. She thought of the house in the pecan grove. Fisher might finish it, but she doubted if he would live there.

Lenore sighed. Anita suspected that Lenore wasn't surprised.

"I think I'd like to learn to run," Lenore said. "You run marathons don't you?"

"No, shorter races," Anita said. "But one of these days I'm going to run a marathon."

"I've got Fisher to thank for it if I do," Lenore said.

They laughed. Anita pictured Lenore practicing on the track.

"But you're sick," Anita said.

Lenore put her hand on Anita's arm and laughed softly.

"I'm going to get well," Lenore said. Lenore paused. "You come stay with me for a while in Memphis. If you want."

"Thanks," Anita said.

But she knew she was not going to stay with Lenore. She was thinking of teaching someplace else where the views were vertical instead of horizontal. A school in the mountains.

It was getting close to dark. Nighthawks swooped and twisted in the air above the trees. Anita thought that she tasted the dog's mouth, even after all those glasses of iced tea, and so she poured another glass and squeezed a lemon into it.

"Let's go to the track," Lenore said.

"You're not well yet," Anita said.

"Just to walk. It's cooling off."

They changed clothes, and Anita drove them to the private school where she taught. Before they got out of the truck they sprayed themselves with mosquito repellent, the sweet cloying scent of it settling on them, turning their skin sticky. Then they went out on the track.

"I learned fast," Lenore said. "It just took a few times. Then I pretended I hadn't learned."

They both laughed.

Lenore walked a white lane marker while Anita held a flashlight so Lenore could see where to put her feet.

"It's still so hot," Lenore said. "Do you think I'll ever be able to run in the heat?"

"Sure," Anita said.

But Anita doubted that Lenore could. She didn't know why, but she thought Lenore belonged in some cold climate, that blond hair spilling out onto a thick wool coat, Lenore's boots crunching on the snow. Perhaps skiing through dark conifers, Anita thought. And this image satisfied her.

Anita handed Lenore the flashlight, thinking that it was just like passing the baton in a relay. Then she ran off on the track, listening to her running shoes make splats on the springy synthetic surface, still a little sticky from the heat. She ran easily, letting the thick air slide in and out of her lungs, her body moving in a familiar pattern, her nylon shorts clinging to her thighs, as she turned one curve and then two and then a third, running toward the light that floated gracefully through the dark.

OVERGROWN WITH LOVE

When Leonard Moss determined to marry Suzanne Frattesi, who'd told him plainly that she wasn't sure about him, he decided to let his land return to the wild. It was an impulsive gesture, but Leonard was desperate. The image of Suzanne was constantly before him: her dark hair, her long legs, her habit of taking her lower lip in her teeth when she was thinking hard about something. At his law office people had noticed that he'd lost some of his famous passion for cases. And to him his colleagues seemed to be people who led the most dull and uninteresting lives. Often he would sit at his desk, the yellow legal pad before him, and instead of writing think of Suzanne: her smile, her perfume, the fabric of her dress. He was in love.

Suzanne was the tall black-haired, brown-eyed great-granddaughter of an Italian who'd come to the Mississippi Delta in the thirties and opened a grocery store. She was writing her dissertation for a degree in conservation. Now she traveled about the Delta for a foundation, trying to persuade farmers not to cut down the trees in the few brakes and patches of hardwoods that were left.

Leonard was not in the habit of falling madly in love. He was thirty-two, and over the years he'd slept with a number of women whom he'd taken to dances at the country club and to football games and to dinner in Memphis. He'd planned to marry when he was thirty-five. Throughout his life he'd carefully mapped out the course it would take, and so far everything had fallen neatly into place. He'd played number one singles on his college tennis team; he'd won a Rhodes scholarship; he'd graduated first in his class from law school. Yet instead of taking the offers of jobs at prestigious firms in Atlanta or New York or Memphis, he'd decided to come home to practice. Leonard was uncomfortable in large cities and, despite his achievements, unsure of himself, so that even when he was in England studying on the scholarship, he had a picture in his mind of climbing the front steps of the Victorian house where the best law firm in Greenville had its offices. Now, as everyone had expected, he'd done brilliant work for the firm and a partnership seemed almost within his reach.

He told her about his intention at dinner in Greenville. He'd planned his delivery carefully, had tried to predict all her possible reactions and what he might say in response to them.

They were eating at a restaurant which specialized in huge steaks and tamales. It wasn't the romantic sort of place he wished. He'd have preferred her cousin John's restaurant near Leland where they served Italian food and there were candles on the tables. She had insisted on coming here. But the steaks were good, and he watched Suzanne polish hers off before he was half through with his. He was too nervous to eat.

"I want to talk to you about my land," he said.

He watched her think for a moment, putting her lower lip between her teeth. Suzanne had a mental map in her head of every piece of land in the Delta. It only took her a moment to find his: the brake running diagonally across one side of it, the Indian mound, and a slough taking a slice out of the northeast corner.

"You can't cut down that brake," she said.

Both of them knew the timber wasn't worth the trouble of cutting, and it was too low to plant.

"I'm not going to cut anything down," he said. "I'm going to let it return to hardwood forest."

That was a term she liked to use, "hardwood forest." She would say, "Once the whole Delta was covered with hardwood forest. Think of what that was like." He called a collection of trees "woods."

"That brake is mainly cypress," she said.

"I mean the whole thousand acres," he said.

"You can't."

"I can afford it."

Letting her know he was doing well wouldn't hurt his chances. But taking the land out of cultivation was a gesture that was both out of character for Leonard and one he really couldn't afford. The act suggested instability, and even though some might be sympathetic because it was done out of love, it hinted at a spontaneity the partners might fear would creep into his preparation for cases. And besides these career considerations, he needed the income from the thousand acres of land.

"That's wonderful," she said. "We'll document it. It can become a model for the rest of the country."

Her eyes were shining. He reached across the table and took her hand. They'd casually slept together. But the way she pressed his hand was more reassuring than any caress she'd given him in bed. It could be a sign that she was already falling in love with him. Again he regretted that they were in the restaurant with plastic tablecloths and neon lights overhead.

It was February, the whole Delta made up of greys and dark browns, the farmers preparing the land for planting. He had at least until spring to change his mind. He thought he'd give her the ring around cotton-planting time.

"I never guessed that you were so interesting," she said. "I thought you were just another Greenville lawyer."

Leonard recalled how they'd talked about books and music. He'd taken her to the ballet, the opera, every performance of the Memphis symphony. He'd never considered himself uninteresting. But he kept these thoughts to himself.

"Now you know I'm not," he said.

"Oh, I'm so proud of you," she said.

She leaned across the table and kissed him.

"Now finish your steak," she said. "Or give it to me."

They split it and asked the waitress for another order of tamales.

They talked about how the land would look as it began to return to the wild: first weeds and then quick growing softwoods and at last the oaks and hickories. Leonard, no farmer himself, had been renting the land out. He liked to return to the house where he'd grown up and sit on the back porch and look out across that perfectly flat land planted with cotton or soybeans and some years sunflowers, stretching away in the distance toward the green smear on the horizon which was the levee.

They talked until the owner had asked them for a third or fourth time whether they wanted anything else. People were waiting for their table.

Outside in the cold they walked with their arms about each other. Leonard thought of how in thirty years they might be coming out of this same restaurant, their children off at college, Suzanne's hair shot through with grey but her beauty incorruptible, her delicate cheekbones, her thin, finely sculptured nose likely to grow more elegant with age. They'd walk to their car, her step steady, her heels clicking on the sidewalk, she moving with the graceful carriage of a dancer. And he would be happy.

Leonard's renter was shocked when Leonard told him of his plans.

"That's gonna be an expensive hunting club," the man said.

"There'll be no hunting allowed," Leonard said.

The man regarded him carefully before he spoke.

"A wildlife sanctuary," he said.

"That's right," Leonard said.

"Remind me not to hire you for a lawyer," the man said. "You'll be too damn expensive."

They both laughed at that, and Leonard was relieved the tension was broken.

Word soon spread about his intentions. Leonard had to put up with jokes at the office. The partners kidded him in their genial way, yet he feared they might be talking seriously about him at firm meetings. But since nothing was growing yet, nobody was that interested. Some hinted they knew why he'd done it. Leonard ignored their innuendoes and double entrendres. He didn't care because he believed Suzanne was now in love with him. Sometimes she called him at the office twice a day just to talk about what the land was going to look like when it began to return to the wild. Leonard yearned for the day when they'd talk about children or houses they wanted to build. Yet for the moment he was happy.

Suzanne was traveling a good deal, but they tried to have lunch or dinner at least once during the week. On the weekends they were constantly together. They met for lunch on a warm day in the middle of February. It felt like spring; jonquils were sprouting in the yards and a few dogwood had been tricked into blooming.

"I want to move out of my apartment," Suzanne said.

Leonard could hardly contain his enthusiasm. He imagined her living with him in his condo. He thought of her clothes in his dresser drawers, her makeup things in the bathroom. But Suzanne wasn't talking. She'd taken a big bite out of her barbecue sandwich.

He took a deep breath and calmed himself.

"There's plenty of room in my condo," he said.

"I know," she said. "That's what I'd like to do. But I want to live at the farm, in your house. I want to be right there to record everything."

"I could move out there too," he said.

He liked the idea of living together in the farmhouse. But she persuaded him that the hour-and-a-half drive to Greenville would be too far.

"You like to work late," she said. "I'd worry about you driving that highway at night."

So Suzanne moved into the old house alone. It was a one-story house built with high ceilings and rooms on either side of a breezeway down the center so that even in the summer it stayed cool.

And in the spring, on a Saturday they'd designated as cotton-planting day, and planned to celebrate with champagne, he gave her the ring. They

sat on the back porch, looking out through the screen at the land stretching away to the levee. His mother's African violet pots were stacked on the
floor in a corner. For a time he'd watered them but finally gave up and
allowed them to shrivel and die. The champagne was iced in a galvanized
bucket his father had used to carry feed to his foxhounds. Suzanne had
moved into his parents' bedroom. Making love to her there always made
him vaguely uncomfortable.

He opened the bottle of champagne. They toasted their project.

"In ten years you won't even be able to see the levee from here," she said.

And he too looked with anticipation to that unbroken stretch of trees,
a dark green wall at the end of the yard beyond the barn.

"I found something today I want you to identify," he said.

He pushed a long spiral-shaped seed pod across the table to her.
Leonard had picked it off a tree in Greenville. She was teaching him the
names of trees. The oaks confused him: pin, white, chinkapin, willow. The
list went on and on, but she knew them all. He was better with grasses and
shrubs. Once she showed him what lespedeza was he never forgot. He liked
to bring her leaves and seedpods to see if she could identify them. He
hadn't stumped her yet.

"A honey locust," she said.

"Do deer eat them?" he asked.

"They love the beans."

"Show me."

She broke open the pod, the ring he'd concealed in an empty bean
pouch falling out onto the table.

"My God," she said.

She leaned back in her chair, her body gone all limp. He watched her
look at the ring on the table and then back at him.

"Put it on," he said.

He was afraid she was going to say no, that she would make some polite
speech ending all his hopes.

But instead, she slipped the ring on her finger and held her hand out to
admire it.

"It's beautiful," she said.

"Are you happy?" he asked.

"How could I not be happy," she said.

She was crying now, a tear working its way down her face.

"Let's go outside," she said.

They stood on the edge of the field, a cold wind coming off it, and
embraced. She said she loved him, and he, looking over her shoulder at

the bare field, the stalks from last year's soybean crop turned grey with bone-white streaks running through them, felt that the loss of the land was a small price to pay.

Johnson grass and cockleburs and cane covered the field by late May. Now that planting time had passed, people who doubted his intentions took the project seriously. Reporters came from the Memphis and Jackson papers. Suzanne cut out the articles. He saved them in a file at his office. Often when he was working late he'd take a break and spread the pieces of ribbon-like newsprint out on his desk. Most of the photographers shot them from a low angle as they stood with their arms about each other, the jungle spreading out behind them.

By the end of June parts of the tangle were head-high. She spent her time measuring the growth of the plants and recording sightings of wildlife: deer, rabbit, racoon, possum. She'd been negotiating with the state fish and game commission for the release of black bear and red wolves onto the land. He didn't think it would work. There was not nearly enough land.

"It'll be just like a virgin forest," she said. "At night we can sit by the fire and listen to the wolves howl."

He'd thought she'd soon tire of the project simply because the forest she envisioned was going to be a long time coming. There'd been times when he'd thought that after their marriage, the date still unset, she might consent to let the land be returned to cultivation. After she saw the bill for the taxes, she might suggest it herself. But for now he planned to be patient and wait.

When he pressed Suzanne about setting a marriage date, she said it would have to be after she delivered a paper to her professional association's meeting in Chicago just after Christmas. It wouldn't be too late, he thought, to have the land bush-hogged and by spring it could be ready for planting. Perhaps the paper would satisfy her.

Suzanne announced that a graduate student in biology wanted to come live at the farm. Leonard wondered if he were some old lover.

"He could live in Greenville," he said.

"Too far," she said.

"Joe Shelby has a trailer he might rent."

She laughed.

"Leonard Moss, are you jealous?"

"Sure, I'm jealous," he said.

"Well, you don't have to be. I'm just doing a favor for the professor who's directing my dissertation."

"Where would he stay?" he asked.

"This house is practically a duplex," she said. "He can stay in your old room. We'll both be working. We'll probably hardly see each other. I'm not even here most of the time."

So he agreed, for he didn't see what else he could do without appearing unreasonable. And when he finally met the student, whose name was Fears, Leonard saw there was nothing to worry about.

Fears was thin, his face covered with pimples, and the only time he didn't look awkward was when he was walking about in the jungle the land had become. Fears never got his feet tangled in vines or his arms scratched by briars. He just seemed to melt into the vegetation as if he were a deer.

He lived in Leonard's old room. On the wall was a map of the farm, divided into grids. Red and blue and yellow pins were stuck in various locations in the squares. Boxes of computer paper were stacked by the window. On the desk was a computer and a printer. Fears never seemed to empty the waste basket, which remained buried beneath a heap of printouts.

Leonard still spent his weekends at the house. Fears had a girlfriend who came to visit him, a small thin girl who never wore makeup and dressed in jeans and sleeveless T-shirts.

By the end of July, Leonard looked at the land and wondered how much it would cost to have it cleared. People at the office had lost interest in making jokes about the project, and Leonard spent considerable energy courting the favor of Mrs. Snead, the office manager, who served as secretary at the firm meetings. She finally told him his project had never been the subject of any formal discussion.

"It's the informal kind I'm worried about," he told her.

"I don't know what passes between the partners informally," she said. "Maybe you should ask the bartender at the country club. That's where they go to talk."

In early August, he got a call from Suzanne, who sounded very excited.

"Come out here," she said. "I have a surprise."

It was Wednesday and he had an important case scheduled to go to trial on Monday. He told her he had to work, but she insisted.

"After you finish," she said.

"I'm going to be here until ten o'clock," he said.

"Try to finish early."

"I don't want to lose the case. I have to work."

"You always do twice as much as is necessary. You come right out. He can't wait."

"Who?"

"I'm sorry. I tried to arrange it for the weekend. But he just showed up. You've got to come right out."

She refused to tell him why she wanted him to come. He finally agreed, deciding he could skip lunch and then return to the office after she showed him whatever it was.

He drove into the yard. A green truck was parked by the barn, a section of steel culvert mounted on the truckbed. A man dressed in a dark green fish and wildlife uniform stood by the truck talking with Suzanne and Fears.

"You're going to be so surprised," Suzanne said.

"You got a bear in there?" he asked. "A wolf?"

Suzanne laughed and refused to answer.

Leonard noticed that the culvert had a sliding door fitted over one end. A large padlock held it in place.

Suzanne and Fears looked at the fish and wildlife man. The three glanced conspiratorially at each other and laughed.

"Tell him, Mr. Luckett," Suzanne said.

"In there is a male and female panther," Mr. Luckett said. "They've come all the way from Florida."

Leonard looked at the jungle, ten feet high now in most places. Here next to the yard pokeweed grew in tall, fleshy profusion, the rank scent of it drifting over them. The insects sang loud and wildly.

"Won't they need more range than a thousand acres?" Leonard asked.

He'd listened to Suzanne and Fears arguing about how many animals and in what numbers the thousand acres could support.

"Fears thinks it'll work," Suzanne said. "He's convinced me."

Then Fears started to talk about population density of deer and the range requirements of panthers.

"If this works it'll be a breakthrough in the introduction of endangered species," he said. "There's already an overpopulation of deer on this land. It'll suit them perfectly."

Fears became excited and waved his hands about as he talked.

"When they begin to reproduce, the population can spill over into the hunting club land along the river," Fears said. "There's miles and miles of habitat there."

Suzanne explained how each animal had been fitted with a collar containing a radio transmitter.

Mr. Luckett got in the truck and backed it up to the edge of the jungle. Fears held the tracking antenna in his hand and wore a set of earphones on his head.

"Right here?" Leonard asked.

"Why not," Suzanne said. "They won't stay around very long."

Leonard thought of the neighbor's house whose roof he could see a quarter of a mile away. He wondered what they were going to say.

Mr. Luckett unlocked the sliding door. Then he climbed on top of the culvert and slowly pulled open the door. Leonard wished he had a rifle in his hands. Suzanne and Fears had assured him the panthers would run for cover, but he wasn't so sure.

A panther stuck its head out the door, something orange around its slate blue neck. The animal hesistated for an instant and then, as if it were a patch of soft blue light and not flesh and blood at all, it disappeared with one bound into the jungle. The other followed. Leonard listened for them moving through the brush, but there was only the rattle from a single pokeweed, its big leaves quivering, and then the insistent hum of the insects.

"Aren't they beautiful?" Suzanne asked.

He admitted they were.

But he was thinking that now the land couldn't be cleared, not as long as the panthers were there. Clearing it would be a death sentence for them. He didn't need the expertise of Suzanne and Fears and Mr. Luckett to tell him that.

Leonard left. They were standing on the front porch. Fears was showing Mr. Luckett and Suzanne his map of the farm. Suzanne looked up and waved to him when he made the turn out of the driveway and onto the road.

The radio transmitters worked well, and Fears spent all his time out in the field keeping track of their movements. The computer drew daily maps of the animals' wanderings, the printouts piling up on the desk and overflowing onto the bed and dresser.

Then Suzanne reported that Fears had stopped finding as many deer kills as usual. And not long after that the panthers began killing dogs. Fears was reluctant to admit the animals had been straying off the overgrown land, but he finally showed Suzanne the maps he'd made, which tallied with reports from people who had seen a panther bounding away into the soybeans or cotton. There were never two, always just one.

Leonard received calls from his neighbors, who wanted the panthers destroyed. The fish and game commission threatened to fine anyone who shot one. Fears had no explanation for their behavior.

Unexpectedly the dog killing stopped, and Fears began to report that the animals had started eating deer again. Suzanne feared the opening of deer season in October. A deer hunter might stray onto their land and kill one of the panthers.

Leonard was working on preparation for a trial with his paralegal, the client's files laid out on the conference table. They heard a commotion in the outer office, and then a man burst into the conference room carrying a plastic garbage bag in his arms. He was unshaven and dressed in a jump suit. Leonard guessed he was a commercial fisherman, a faint odor of fish and river mud hanging about the man.

"You Leonard Moss?" the man asked.

By this time Mrs. Snead and one of the partners had appeared in the doorway behind them. Leonard heard someone saying something about calling the police.

"I am," Leonard said.

The man strode to the conference table and dumped the contents of the garbage bag onto it. Mrs. Snead screamed. Leonard heard someone in the doorway curse. On the table was the partially eaten carcass of a beagle. From Fears, Leonard knew exactly how panthers killed their prey, biting it in the neck, forcing apart the vertebrae and breaking the spinal cord. Then the panther had torn open the abdominal cavity and eaten the dog's liver, heart, and lungs.

"Them Florida panthers killed my dog," the man said. "You ketch 'em, send 'em on back there. Or you'll hear from me again."

Then he left the office, the smell of fish lingering behind him.

Afterward one of the partners, Vickers Malone, took the shaken Leonard for a drink.

"You've got to do something," Vickers said.

Leonard had always admired Vickers, who had just turned sixty. It was a privilege to sit in a courtroom and watch him play to a jury.

"What?" Leonard asked.

"You've got to find out if that Frattesi girl loves you or that thousand acres," Vickers said.

Leonard wasn't surprised that Vickers understood it all so clearly.

"It's too late to do anything," Leonard said.

"That dog may be the last straw for some of the partners," Vickers said. "Deer season opens next weekend. You go hunt on your place. You take care of those animals. Things could turn out better if cotton and beans are growing there next spring."

Vickers told him to take the rest of the day off. Most of the work had been done on the case, and Leonard could finish that the next day. Leonard retreated to a bar where he sat alone, drinking bottled water and considering what Suzanne would do if he shot the panthers and put his place back under cultivation.

He wondered if she really loved him, if she were going to marry him after she gave her paper in Chicago. He tried to imagine her out of his life but couldn't. Over and over he rearranged the pieces: Suzanne, the firm, the panther, the overgrown land. But no combination seemed satisfactory. He felt beaten, drained, and switched from bottled water to whiskey. By the time he walked out of the bar, he knew he was too drunk to drive himself home. So he went to the office and spent the night on the cot he kept there.

On opening day of deer season Leonard rose in the early morning darkness and drove to the house. He arrived just before dawn, the sky a pale rose above the jungle. The light in his old room was on. He supposed that Fears had stayed up all night running his observations on the panthers through his computer.

He decided to sneak a look at Fears' map, which would give him a clear picture of the panthers' movements. He'd tell Fears that he was going deer hunting over on the land beyond the levee, and the man would never suspect a thing. He'd say that he saw the light and had stopped in for a cup of coffee.

Leonard parked in the yard well away from the house. He didn't want to wake Suzanne, who liked to sleep late. Carefully he unlocked the front door and walked slowly across the floorboards, avoiding the one a little left from center that always creaked. There was a sound coming from Fears' room, a heavy rhymthic sound, accompanied by a whistling noise.

He pushed open the door and found Fears jumping rope. The computer terminal was on, displaying a map. Fears smiled at him, his lips moving. Fears was counting. The room was in total disarray: wadded up printouts on the floor, books, clothes, and Fears' radio antenna hanging from one of the hooks in the the ceiling where Leonard had once displayed his model airlanes.

Fears finished but it took a moment for him to catch his breath.

"Five hundred," Fears said. "How many can you do?"

Leonard said he wasn't sure. He looked at the map of the farm on the wall. It was filled with colored pins and wide black lines and circles and squares and rectangles of different colors.

"I got some good data on those panthers," Fears said.

"People are saying there's only one left," Leonard said.

"That's true," Fears said.

Fears explained that the male had been killed but that he hoped the female was pregnant. She'd recently made a den on the banks of the slough.

Leonard thought of the panthers multiplying. He might never get rid of them.

"How many would she have?" Leonard asked.

"Four to six," Fears said. "Those kittens would provide breeding stock."

Fears asked Leonard why he'd come out so early.

"Deer season," Leonard said.

"I've seen a couple of big bucks," Fears said.

He took Leonard to the map and pointed out the places he'd seen the deer.

Leonard looked at the map. The triangles and circles and squares were to him the same as undecipherable Mayan glyphs. He stared at the map, the key to his salvation. He thought of the partnership he'd worked so hard to attain.

"You can see her on your way to hunt that buck," Fears said.

Fears told him that the den was under a fallen cypress. Leonard knew the place. Fears had constructed a blind on the opposite side of the slough where he could observe her.

"You just can't tell anyone," Fears said. "But you're the one who provided the land. You've got a right to see her. In a way she's your panther."

Fears saying that made Leonard uncomfortable. The land was his, but not the panther. Leonard thought of the energy Fears had devoted to the project and of Suzanne asleep in his parents' bed.

"You better get moving," Fears said. "Sun is already up."

Leonard left the house quietly. He was glad he hadn't had to face Suzanne.

Leonard followed a game trail to the slough and then walked upstream along its east bank until he came upon the blind made of camouflage netting stretched over an aluminum frame. By good luck he was downwind from the den. He moved carefully into the blind, checking the ground for snakes. Through the tiny window he saw the fallen cypress two hundred yards away.

He slipped the rifle through the window and put the telescopic sight on the cypress. The grass had been beaten down around the den, but he saw no sign of the female. So he sat on the ground, his eye to the sight, and waited. It was going to be a cloudless late October day. The dark water of the slough glittered under the morning sun. A gar rolled, gulping air, a turtle crawled up on a log, the insects whined from the grass. Once from far away in the direction of the levee he heard the report of a rifle.

He waited an hour, then two. A mosquito, somehow immune to the insect repellent, buzzed in his ear, but he didn't slap at it, afraid to make some noise the panther might hear. It fed on him until, filled with blood, it flew away. Another hour passed; his legs ached from sitting.

Still the space before the den was empty. He tried not to think about the time that had passed; he tried not to think of time at all. But he was growing stiff, the edge of the scope pressing uncomfortably around his eye. He took his eye from the scope. As he rubbed the place where it had irritated his skin, he looked back down the trail. And there was the panther. She sat in an open space, motionless except for the twitching of her tail. She looked lean and fit.

He brought up the rifle slowly. She didn't move. He put his eye to the scope, her body filling it, so there was not the jungle or water or sky in it but only the panther. He saw the individual blue hairs of her coat and a deertick engorged with blood. But he wasn't sure exactly where he was shooting. He didn't want to put a round into her belly; he didn't want her to suffer. Taking his eye from the scope, he looked under it along the barrel of the rifle. He imagined the path of the bullet out of the barrel and into her shoulder, the slug breaking bones and finding, if he were lucky, her heart and lungs. *Run, damn you,* he thought. *Run.* He took a deep breath and moved his finger to take up the slack on the trigger, preparing to release the air slowly as he squeezed it. He thought of Vickers' hand on his shoulder, the fatherly pat, as the older man gave his sensible advice. He thought of Suzanne, who was probably having breakfast on the porch, and of Fears studying a printout in the bedroom. The panther's tail had stopped twitching. He lowered the rifle.

He yelled, not a human sound at all, inarticulate and coming from deep in his belly. The panther melted into the tangle. He listened for the sound of its paws on the leaves but there was nothing. He looked at the open space and it was as if the panther had never been there at all.

He regarded the jungle and thought: *This is what I have chosen.* He imagined the plants sinking their roots deep into the soil, that richness transformed into leaf and branch utterly without commercial value. The oaks and hickories would take fifty years or so to grow large enough to be sold. If his law practice didn't prosper, the land could be sold for taxes he'd be unable to pay. He pictured himself putting the land back under cultivation and what she would think of that.

And he thought of himself starting over in some small office with a single secretary. He imagined he might rent the empty rooms above the hardware store where there was a balcony looking out on the street. There was a skylight because once it had been used for grading cotton. He'd put his desk under that and work all day bathed in natural light.

The partners would laugh about him over drinks at the country club. They'd tell jokes about Leonard Moss, the Greenville lawyer, who one day let his carefully planned life fall into confusion, who for love let his well-tended farm return to the wild. He wondered if Suzanne would end up changing her mind about him. His life was not going to be an easy one, no romance in struggling for clients. If she stopped loving him, it wouldn't be worth it at all.

Leonard got up and left the blind carefully, keeping it between himself and the den. For a time he had to push his way through the tangle, briars catching at his clothes, but then he found a game trail and the walking was easy. He held the rifle in front to him to break the spider webs, some still glistening with drops of dew. If he hurried he'd be able to have breakfast with Suzanne, and then as they sat amid the debris of the meal—biscuit crumbs, jam, half-empty coffee cups—he'd tell her of his plans for his office and spend the rest of the day leisurly nurturing their love, imagining its growth—as splendid and lush and mysterious as that thick green jungle.

A ROBBER'S TALE

I came to France to rob trains. One day, while I was still in high school, I felt the urge begin to sing in my blood, a persistent whine, like cicadas at the end of a long, hot summer. Maybe it was because my kin rode with Jesse James in Kansas and Missouri. I tried to pay it no mind, but it wouldn't go away. It was like Brother Carnes's call to preach he always talks about, something you just can't ignore. In the States there're no trains left worth robbing. Who'd want to hold up an AmTrak? So here I am in France where trains are still respected institutions.

On my passport it says my name is Robert Quincy Vernon. It also says I'm twenty years old. The photo is of a man with a smile on his face, his brown hair cut short, his green eyes looking into the camera like he don't think much of whoever's taking the picture. The passport is stamped with a student visa. If you asked someone who knows Robert Quincy, they'd tell you he weighs about 170 pounds and stands six-feet-and-one-inch tall. They'd tell you he was born in Mountain Home, Arkansas, and attended the University of Arkansas. They'd tell you he's spending his junior year abroad studying French in Aix-en-Provence.

I know these things because Robert Quincy and I grew up together. We fished for smallmouth, hunted, played football, smoked marijuana from my cousin Lonnie's field, made love to girls with names like Nona, Lillie, and Mary Lee on moonlit sandbars on the Buffalo River, things like you do if you grow up around Mountain Home. Robert Quincy usually had those girls first. I got his leavings.

Robert Quincy had them first because he's beautiful, not a word I'd ordinarily apply to a man. I think of him putting on his pads in the locker room, and I understand why I always lost out to him. I lifted weights to build myself up. Robert Quincy was born with that chest, the muscles laid up under his skin in smooth slabs.

My name is Billy Wells. I'm almost six-three, and my eyes are more blue than green. But there's a likeness between Robert Quincy's passport photo and the unsmiling picture on my military ID. Sometimes I wonder. Robert Quincy's daddy has a reputation with the ladies. Once or twice after a football game I'd come out of our dressing room, a cinder-block building with a cottonmouth coiled and ready to strike painted on the side, and see the old man and my mother talking, standing there alone by the ticket stand. It's crossed my mind that Robert Quincy and I could be half-brothers.

My father was home from Saudi Arabia when Mother got pregnant with me. At least that's what she says. Then my daddy went back to the desert to fight an oil well fire and got himself killed. He'd been away for four months and was only home for two weeks before he left. It had been like that the whole time they were married. Mr. Vernon had all the opportunities, not my daddy.

I got a trip to Europe too, just like Robert Quincy, but the army, not my rich family, paid my fare. I told everyone I was joining up because I wanted to save money for college. I did real good on the army language test. So they decided to teach me Russian. Only now there's not much use for that because of the end of the cold war. I didn't feel bad about going AWOL.

Robert Quincy was surprised when I showed up in France. He gave me his passport, money, and a credit card. I didn't even have to ask. It wasn't him feeling bad about all those girls. He's been like that his whole life. Generous. Robert Quincy said he'd wait awhile and report the passport stolen. He expected I'd be out of Europe and home by then.

Right now I'm standing on a scrub oak–covered slope in the foothills of the Pyrenees above the railroad tracks which run from the town of Quillan to Carcassone. The countryside reminds me a little of the western edge of the Ozarks: dry, the trees a little stunted. The tracks for the little commuter train follow the Aude as it snakes through the mountains. Out on the tracks, at the top of a steep grade, I've stacked some logs soaked in gasoline. I threw an old tire on top for good measure. It'll make plenty of thick black smoke and confuse the engineer.

I check the pair of Navy Colts I've got stuck in my belt. I bought 'em at an open-air market. Who knows where that Frenchman got 'em? He swore they're the real thing. Jesse might have used a pair just like them. I think of him and his brother Frank, riding round that tree they practiced on when they were boys, girdling it with bullets. They probably knew that soon, with the war coming on, they'd be shooting at men instead of trees.

Me and that Frenchman went into an alley to conclude the sale. He was worried about the gendarmes. He threw in two boxes of shells for free.

I hear the little three-car train coming up the grade. It's a disappointment to me that it's not a steam engine, but you can't have everything. I walk over to the pile of logs and flip my cigarette into it. The gasoline goes up with a whoosh. I step back from the heat. The tire is a great success. It produces a dense black, oily-looking smoke.

I adjust my cowboy hat, pulling it down low over my eyes, and tie a black bandanna over my face. I'm wearing a cattleman's long slicker, although it's a hot day. But it'll be good for disguise. They won't see anything but my eyes. Then I put the fire between me and the approaching train, careful not to scuff my snakeskin boots on the rocks.

The train stops, the brakes squeal. I have to work quickly because that engineer will be on the radio to someone fast. Robbers had it easier in the old days. I walk out from behind the burning pile of logs, holding a heavy Colt in each hand.

There are three of them: a conductor and two engineers, all dressed in the blue caps of the SNCF, the French railroad system. The conductor wears a tie.

"*Attention, Monsieurs!*" I say.

After learning Russian, picking some French up was easy.

The conductor shakes his head. One of the engineers folds his arms. The other laughs. Passengers have stuck their heads out of the windows. There are not many. The train is nearly empty.

"*En haut!*" I say, "*En haut.*"

I motion with the barrels of the Colts.

They understand the gesture. Probably from all the American TV they watch. They slowly put their hands up but not very high. The conductor sticks both his hands in his pockets.

Things aren't going well. These folks aren't taking me seriously. Once a man Jesse robbed complained of the quality of Jesse's horse, said that when he was in the Confederate cavalry, he wouldn't be caught dead riding such an animal. Instead of shooting him for the insult, Jesse returned his gold watch and his money. He didn't rob fellow veterans.

I consider shooting the conductor's hat off, a good start on my own legend, but worry about my marksmanship. So I put a bullet between the conductor's feet, the Colt bucking in my hand. Their hands shoot up. A woman passenger screams. Then they understand. They are being robbed.

The passengers stand in a line by the car. There are six of them. A mother and her daughter, a farmer with chickens in a cage, a stout middle-aged woman holding an empty market basket against her breasts, and two kids.

"Texas! Texas!" the two kids keep saying and laughing.

The passengers are a little like my people in Arkansas, obviously hard-working, with not much of a chance of doing anything the rest of their lives but sweating for somebody else. You'd think I'd send them on their way. I rob them anyway. Jesse would have done the same and maybe recited them a Bible verse.

I take their rings and watches. One woman wears a gold locket on a silver chain. I take that too. The frightened farmer offers me the chickens, but I politely refuse. I want portable wealth. I take the kids' soccer ball because they keep jumping around and refuse to stand in line. And I take all the money. Everything I place in a plastic garbage bag.

"*Au revoir, madames et monsieurs. Et enfants,*" I say. "*Merci.*"

No one says anything in reply. The kids are crying because of the soccer ball. Only the conductor and the engineer have kept their hands raised.

I back off up the slope, covering them with the revolvers, until I reach the trees. I wish I had a horse. I had thought of stealing one to make my escape, but they'll have gendarmes on the roads, probably even a helicopter airborne in a few minutes. I pause and look down at the train. They're standing about looking up at me. I take the soccer ball out of the bag and toss it down the slope, the ball bouncing in a huge arc off a rock and through the limbs of a tree, where I'm afraid it'll get stuck, but it finally clears them and rolls up against the side of the train. The kids wave to me. I wave back.

Up on the mountain I hide the valuables that can be identified in a cave. I keep the money. Then I change into hiking boots, shorts, and a shirt. I stuff my outlaw clothes into another plastic bag. I've bought an internal frame backpack and camping gear. Now I'm Robert Quincy again.

Of course I get picked up by the gendarmes. I'm walking a ridgeline when a helicopter swoops down on me. They look at my passport and question me about the cowboy robber. They poke around in my backpack, but it just has the usual things: stove, dehydrated food, rain gear, a tent, a down sleeping bag, a change of clothes. I tell them I'm touring Cathar chateaux in the area and plan to be around for a while. I know the next time is not going to be so easy.

In Carcassone I use Robert Quincy's credit card to buy a mountain bike. I'm tired of walking. And I have a girl friend. Her name is Natalie. She has dark eyes and hair. When she laughs, she tosses her head, her short, glossy hair rippling like a horse's mane, her lips making a kind of pout just before they open. Women don't laugh like that in Arkansas. I sat down next to Natalie in a cafe one day and started talking to her. I didn't expect her to fall in love with me. But she did. Now it's like there are two sets of voices inside my head, one urging me to rob trains and the other talking soft and seductive, telling me that I should forget about trains and keep myself close to Natalie. Maybe it was like that for Jesse. But when it came time to rob, he was there, a Navy Colt in his hand.

We meet in that same cafe. I drink beer with her, looking over her shoulder at the battlements of the old walled city set on a hill across the Aude, the river considerably wider now. The towers rise into the blue sky like a fairy tale castle.

Natalie is home for the summer from school. She's attending the university at Toulouse where she's studying to be a civil engineer. We make love in my hotel room next to the railroad station, the room paid for by the money I stole from the passengers. The Canal du Midi is right outside my window.

"Robert, it is so sad you have to return to Aix," she says.

"We both have our studies," I say.

I enjoy playing the role of a student. But I have to stay alert. She keeps mentioning American books she assumes I've read.

"Will you visit me?" she asks.

She offers me a cigarette; I shake my head. She smokes them fast, hardly seeming to draw the smoke into her lungs.

"Yes."

"Do you love me?"

I tell her I do. And that soft voice in my head purrs.

"Next summer we can take a trip on the canal," she says.

I wonder if I can stay here until next summer. Sooner or later the army's Criminal Investigation Division people will pay a visit to Robert Quincy. Those CID boys are sharp. They'll go to Arkansas, talk to all my friends. In Germany we monitered Russian military radio traffic, all top secret stuff. Having me on the loose will make everyone nervous.

"We could rent a houseboat," I say.

I think of sitting with her in the evening, the boat moored to a plane tree.

"Yes," she says.

She begins to explain how the canal's system of locks works. I listen politely, enjoying her excitement as she describes the machinery. Then we make love again. The way she touches my body, as if it belongs to an old familiar lover, makes me want to stay in Carcassone forever.

My second train is on the line from Aix-le-Therme to Foix. I'm not ready for the Toulouse to Paris line. It's going to be difficult to stop a train going over a hundred and fifty kilometers an hour. And it's likely to be filled with young French paratroopers in red berets. They're sure to be troublesome. This four-car train on a mid-week run is much safer. It'll be like diving off a cliff into the Buffalo River. You work up gradually, one ledge at a time, and by the end of the summer you're standing on top, the drop into the pool of clear green water not seeming so bad at all.

I stop the train by stealing a car, a yellow Deux Chevaux, and parking it on the tracks. Things go badly. The engineer can't quite get the train stopped and it crashes into the car. Although the train is traveling very slowly, the impact carries the car along the tracks for at least fifty meters.

While the train crew is dealing with the crash, I enter the last car. No one is hurt, but a suitcase has burst open and there are clothes scattered on the floor. A girl, very young and very thin, is picking up a pair of sequined jeans and stuffing them back into the suitcase. Her back is to me. Her two friends, who are the only other passengers in the car, their lips painted an apple red and patches of blush on their cheekbones, have looks of amazement on their faces. I'm pleased.

"Texas!" the girls scream. "Texas!"

I line them up at the end of the car and take their money. Only a few francs. They look very sad when I put the money in my garbage bag. But a train robber can't afford to be sentimental.

Then I'm out of the car and scrambling up the side of the mountain through the scrub oak and thorn bushes. The conductor gives chase, along with a few passengers. But when I fire a couple of shots in the air, they abandon me to the gendarmes. I hide the clothes and the Colts.

I ride the mountain bike over a trail which connects with a road. I think of Natalie and I wonder how Jesse felt about such distractions. Amazingly, the gendarmes miss me. I sit in a cafe on the highway and drink *kir,* the drink sweeter because it was bought with stolen money. I listen to the patrons speculate on what is happening. Five cars, their klaxons blaring and blue lights flashing, have already passed. I finish my beer and ride off.

After spending the night in my tent in the forest, I ride into Carcassone and call Natalie. She tells me we'll meet in a friend's apartment.

The apartment is decorated with travel posters on the walls: Saint Tropez, Guadeloupe, Rome. There's an umbrella tied over the ceiling light as a shade.

I'm tired of being Robert Quincy. I'm starting to worry if I can ever be Billy Wells again, part of Robert Quincy mixed up in me forever. So I tell her who I really am, a deserter from the United States Army. She laughs. She doesn't believe me. Then I show her the passport. She takes a long look at it, glancing back and forth from the picture to me.

"It is true," she says.

I think of Robert Quincy sitting in a cafe in Aix, watching women walk up and down the plane tree–lined main street in short dresses.

"We'll go to Aix," I say.

"Why?" she asks.

"To give Robert Quincy his passport back. I don't want to be him anymore."

"Good."

We take an early morning train. We walk through the morning streets of Carcassone, the chain link screens over the shop windows still padlocked. The streets are wet from a recent cleaning, the puddles shining in the bright sunlight. I cross the canal and pause on the bridge. On the bank a yacht is set up on blocks, its hull in the process of being repainted. I think of slowly navigating the canal in the boat with Natalie, the towpath marked with plane trees, the canal running in smooth curves through vineyards and fields of corn.

On the train Natalie sits with her arms around my neck. The train starts off with a lurch and gets up to speed, the green fields and trees rippling past. She kisses me. I think of how difficult it would be to rob this train.

Aix shimmers in the sun. We drink beer in the shade of a cafe awning before going to Robert Quincy's. He has an apartment on rue Voltaire.

"Damn, Billy, you're supposed to be in Arkansas," Robert Quincy says when he opens the door.

We sit on the little balcony overlooking the street and drink beer. Natalie has gone out to buy something for supper. Robert Quincy has been looking her over good. He wants to talk about Natalie, but I don't let him. I tell him about the trains.

"You better get yourself out of France," Robert Quincy says.

"First I'm gonna rob the TGV," I say.

Robert Quincy laughs.

"Not that one," he says. "How you gonna stop something like that."

The TGV is the high-speed train that runs between Paris and Marseilles. It's the jewel of France.

"That girl know about those trains?" Robert Quincy asks.

I shake my head. Voices drift up to us from the street.

"Once I get her to Arkansas it won't matter," I say.

Robert Quincy laughs again. It the same kind of laugh he might give if he'd just hit my best fastball over the fence, laughing and jogging around the bases. The sunlight falls on him, his shirt open at the collar, the hair on his arms and chest looking like gold wires.

"She won't go back with you," Robert Quincy says. "You don't understand French girls."

"Maybe I do," I say.

"Have it your way then."

Natalie comes back and cooks us duck for dinner. I talk to her in English and Robert Quincy talks to her in French. She laughs at his French, but I think she understands almost everything he says. She sits on my lap and talks with him. We all drink plenty of wine.

In bed with Natalie I think of how the army will catch me sooner or later. But even after they give me a dishonorable discharge, I can still get a job in Arkansas raising chickens or cutting pulp wood. Nobody will ever know it was me who robbed those trains. I go to sleep with her in my arms.

I wake and reach out for Natalie, but find the bed empty. No noise rises up from the street through the open window. I lie there on my back and wait for her to return. Maybe she's just gone to the bathroom. But she doesn't come back.

I get up and walk out of the bedroom. I trip over a wine bottle in the living room, but it doesn't fall, just wobbles on its base against the tile floor. Then out on the balcony I see them. She sits on the wall, her head thrown back and her eyes closed. Robert Quincy stands between her legs, the muscles of his buttocks tightened as he moves slowly in her. Her fingertips play across his back.

I pretend to be asleep when she lies down again beside me. I think I can smell the scent of Robert Quincy on her as she runs a hand across my back. Almost immediately she falls asleep. I get up and quietly leave the bedroom.

It's when I'm crossing the living room, careful to avoid the wine bottle, that I see Robert Quincy on the balcony, sitting on the wall where Natalie sat. He brings a cigarette to his mouth, the tip making a glowing arc in the darkness. I go out to the balcony.

"You leaving?" Robert Quincy asks.

"I reckon," I say.

Then there's a long silence. I hear a hum off on the street. Maybe a power pole transformer that's getting ready to fail.

"I'm sorry," he says.

"Don't be," I say.

"She came to my bedroom. I told you about those French girls."

"Same as those in Arkansas."

He laughs.

"Billy, what are you doing?" he asks.

"Practicing to rob the TGV," I say.

"You gonna go to jail."

"They won't catch me."

"And after you rob it. What then?"

"I ain't thought that far ahead."

I think of trying to explain to him how it feels to rob a train. Robert Quincy wouldn't understand. He's free to do what he wants. I can work in a chicken plant, drive a truck, or cut pulpwood. That's about all. But when I'm standing on the tracks, the Colts in my hand, I sail free of all of it. The TGV. That train will take me to a place beyond what I could describe in words.

"You watch yourself," he says.

"You too," I say. "Can't trust them French girls."

We both laugh.

He puts his hand on my shoulder.

"You can come back here," he says.

"I won't be back," I say.

We shake hands. I turn and walk back through the apartment, leaving him sitting on the wall.

I walk through the deserted streets toward the train station.

Robert Quincy has taken her off my hands, the only time something like that has happened when I wanted it to happen. If I'd stayed with her, I'd have ended up floating down that canal, a beautiful but pointless thing to do.

Now I'm free to rob the TGV. I think of watching the train come up the tracks. Waiters will be working in the dining car, serving champagne and oysters. And I'll be waiting with those Navy Colts, the train coming on and on, making a heavy sound, until the engineer sees me standing astride the rails, a phantom in a yellow slicker who'll take from the passengers jewels and Rolex watches and those big French banknotes.

I imagine Robert Quincy practicing law in Arkansas. I imagine his wife and children. I imagine his mistresses. I imagine his unhappiness and dissatisfaction as he grows older. Maybe from time to time he'll think of a few weeks in Aix he spent with a girl named Natalie.

And me? I'll be in those Frenchmen's heads, but not as an insubstantial airy thing. No dream. I'll be like the vibration from the rails that runs through the passengers' bodies, as real as the blood that pumps through their veins: boots and slicker and hat and Navy Colts, standing tall, waiting for them as they turn the corner into Texas.

NIGHT VISION

John Emory stood on the asphalt with the other soldiers and shivered in the cold. Someone had stolen his field jacket while he slept on a bench at Cam Rahn Bay. He stayed out of the shade of the big spruces, but the bright late afternoon sunlight, shooting down out of a cloudless blue sky, offered little warmth. Off to the west snow-covered Mt. Ranier towered above Fort Lewis. The men milled about, smoked, complained of the wait. A medic stepped out onto the porch of the hospital. The soldiers had just completed their separation physicals.

"You men will be brought back here tomorrow," he said. Then he grinned. "Your blood tests are all fucked up."

The men groaned. Everyone was thinking of syphilis. The men talked nervously about it. The story of the island in the Pacific where they sent you, never to return, when you contracted an incurable Eastern strain of the disease, was brought out again and discussed. Emory thought of the girls in Pleiku, the girls in Singapore.

"It's the black syph," a soldier said.

Emory recalled that the man's chest was covered with schrapnel scars, a crisscrossed pattern of welts. The doctor had asked him if they itched. The man's skin was very white, and the welts were still an angry reddish color. Emory had come out of the war without a scratch; he hadn't killed anyone. Once he had thought not having killed would bother him, a missed rite of initiation. In training a drill sergeant often repeated as a kind of litany to the assembled men: "I have killed. I have killed," the words spoken in a flat emotionless voice. But instead of regret, Emory felt a great sense of relief, even of joy. The war hadn't touched him. He would go home to Mobile; everything would be exactly as it was before he left.

The medic lingered on the porch and answered their questions.

"I ain't fucking with you," he finally said. "That sorry-ass machine broke again. Happens all the time. Why, all your dicks are probably just as clean as mine."

He laughed and disappeared into the hospital.

The buses arrived. Emory settled into his seat, grateful for the warmth, as his bus drove about the post. By this time tomorrow he might be in Mobile. He imagined calling up girls he had known in high school, now in college, and asking them for a date. Around dusk he'd stroll up to one of those houses set amid magnolias and live oaks and pines, a brick sidewalk under the soles of his cordovans. After speaking with a girl's parents, he'd walk his date out to the car in that warm April or May air. They'd go to a movie; they'd have dinner. In the fall he was going off to college himself.

The driver stopped in front of one barracks after another and called the men's names off a list. They departed the bus in twos and threes. Finally only Emory, who had already fallen asleep twice, was left. It was getting late, the sun dropping down behind the spruces, but the snow fields on the volcano still shone in the light.

Emory picked up his duffel bag and went off the bus. The driver motioned with his head toward the barracks.

"They got the dishonorable discharges in there," he said. "Waiting for their paperwork. Then they'll get a free ride to the front gate."

The driver laughed.

"I wouldn't want to sleep there," he said. "Those guys do whatever they want."

"I don't care where I sleep," Emory said.

"Yeah, you infantry guys just don't give a shit," the driver said.

Neither of them laughed.

Emory got off the bus. It pulled away. The driver waved to him, but Emory didn't wave back. He'd listened to enough jokes about his trade from clerks and drivers to last him a long time.

He stood in the cold and looked at the barracks, no different from any of the others on the post. He went up the walk, the bag over his shoulder. He anticipated the pleasure of stretching out on a bunk and dropping off to sleep.

When he pushed open the door, the music washed over him. Someone was playing a radio turned up very high. Men dressed in civilian clothes lay about on the bunks; the odor of marijuana was in the air. There were plenty of empty bunks, and Emory wondered why they hadn't sent everyone to this barracks. He took a bunk in a corner, although he had given up on the idea of going to sleep.

On the bunk beside him a little man dressed in a fringed leather jacket sat playing cards with a big man who wore a pair of bell-bottomed jeans and a paisley shirt with pearl buttons. Both wore cowboy boots. A pile of bills was beside the little man, but the big man was down to a few bills and some change. They concentrated on their game and ignored Emory.

"Will you watch my stuff?" Emory asked. "I've got to go to the orderly room."

"What you going over there for?" the big man asked.

"To get some sheets and a blanket," Emory said.

"Listen at that, Arnold," the little man said to the big man.

Arnold laughed.

"I'd like to have some sheets myself," he said.

"And a pillow," the little man said.

"Prince has been down there every day to complain," Arnold said. "They won't do nothing for us."

"We've got our rights," Prince said. "They're gonna be sorry. I'm writing my congressman."

"Go do it then," Arnold said. Then he turned back to Emory. "Where'd you come from."

"Vietnam," Emory said.

"What'd you do," Prince asked.

"Infantry," Emory said.

"I was infantry," Arnold said.

"I kept my ass out of Vietnam," Prince said.

Arnold told Emory he was going back to Texas and work on his father's ranch. The ranch was in the hill country. Arnold talked about the beauty of the hills and how he planned to take a packhorse and camp in a grove of oaks beside a river to get the smell of the army off him.

"He's gonna catch trout," Prince said.

"Ain't no trout in Texas," Arnold said.

"Catfish then," Prince said. "Arnold says I can come down there sometime. He'll teach me to ride."

"Maybe," Arnold said.

Arnold was going to raise and train cutting horses. On his father's ranch it wouldn't matter he had been court-martialed for hitting a sergeant.

"I been to Vietnam," Arnold said. "I got back here and they started fucking with me."

"Wish I had me someplace to go like that," Prince said.

Prince wanted to get a job driving cars across the country from New York. He was from New Jersey. Prince hadn't made it through basic training.

"I wouldn't do shit for them," he said. "I told 'em my balls hurt. They ain't got a test for that. Drill sergeant cussed and threw rocks at me, but I wouldn't move. They say I'm an undesirable."

Prince grinned.

Emory managed a smile. He was almost free of the army. Soon he would no longer have to live with people like Prince and Arnold.

"I'm going to get some sheets," Emory said.

They laughed.

"They won't give you nothing," Arnold said. "But if they do you get us some too."

Emory walked into the orderly room. It had turned colder, and he buttoned his jungle fatigues at the collar. A staff sergeant sat behind a desk. He asked for sheets and a blanket. The sergeant requested his barracks number.

"No sheets in that barracks," the sergeant said. "What're you doing there?"

Emory explained about the blood test.

"Sorry," the sergeant said. "I can give you a blanket but no sheets. They're bad on sheets."

"You can give them to me," Emory said.

The sergeant shook his head.

"Give out a set to one and all of 'em be in here wanting some," he said.

Emory asked to be put in another barracks. The sergeant made some calls.

"There's nothing," he said. "I'd watch myself over there. That's a rough bunch."

Emory took his blanket and, wrapping it about him, walked back to the barracks.

Arnold and Prince were gone when he returned, but no one had stolen his duffel bag. Emory thought of returning to the orderly room and volunteering for guard duty, but he was so sleepy he didn't think he would stay awake. He could end up getting court-martialed himself for falling asleep.

So he took off his shoes, stuffed his billfold between his underwear and his skin, and, putting one arm through the duffel bag's strap, lay down to sleep.

He slept and dreamed of the outpost, located high on a mountaintop outside of Pleiku where he had spent twelve months. It was just two squads up there. At night he watched the ridge below through a starlight scope and listened to the geckos bark. Sometimes the nights were cold, especially during the dry season. When the monsoon came, the wind blew constantly, driving a cold rain to rattle against his poncho.

In his dream he kept seeing movement in the dark. As he stared hard into the darkness, bushes and rocks began to move. The army taught you a trick to keep that from happening. You looked to the side of things and not directly at them. Then they'd stop moving. No matter what he did the bushes and rocks started walking. He'd get scared and fire off a burst at what he thought was an enemy soldier. Finally the squad leader made him stand watch with only a .45. That way something would have to be very close before he'd be tempted to open fire.

"The night is always walking for Emory," the squad leader liked to say.

Yet in all that time he hadn't killed anyone. In the morning the targets he'd fired at during the night turned out to be rocks and trees. It was as if the North Vietnamese Army had chosen to ignore the outpost as not worth the trouble of harassing.

During bad weather he worried because they were cut off from gunship support. When that happened and the mountain top was hidden in the clouds, he'd be too scared to sleep, and he'd stay up all night, staring off into the clouds, which rolled through the concertina wire, grey pieces of cloud seeming to be caught up on the barbs and torn apart. At those times he knew a platoon of NVA could have overrun them in an hour.

Lost in one of these night-vision dreams, his body prickly with fear, Emory woke with a start. Two men were fighting on the floor. A light black man was beating a dark one with a stick, the club making a solid sound on the other man's head.

Arnold and Prince had returned. They both sat on the top bunk, and like the rest of the men in the barracks were silent as the fight went on. Finally the darker man lay still on the floor, the man with the stick standing over him. He was dressed in a suit; the man on the floor wore a warmup.

"You stay out of my locker, motherfucker," the man said.

The loser said nothing in reply. He groaned, twisting his body into a fetal position.

The winner walked off, and two men helped the defeated man into the latrine. Emory had seen fights before, but somehow this one made him nervous. He supposed it was because everyone had been so quiet, and there

was no sergeant or lieutenant on hand to break it up. He suspected that
the light-skinned man could still be beating the barracks thief and no one
would've made a move to stop him.

"Fucking Hardin is always in everyone's shit," Prince said.

"Hey, Emory," Arnold said. "We got some speed. Nobody sleeps at
night in this barracks. You come fly with us."

Emory told them no. He was going to sleep anyway.

"I was in the Delta," Arnold said. "I could shoot a fifty caliber from the
hip. Everyone was safe when I was around. You ever seen a slope that's
been greased with a fifty?"

Emory said he hadn't.

Arnold went on and on about his exploits in the Delta. Emory imagined the big man with the heavy machine gun, meant to be mounted on
a jeep or fired from a tripod, in his hands.

"You are full of shit," a voice said.

Emory looked up. The man in the suit was standing at the end of the
bunk. He still had his long delicate fingers wrapped around the club,
which was the butt end of a pool cue.

"Arnold wasn't in no Vietnam," the man said. "Shit, he didn't even
finish basic."

"Fieldspar, how come you know everthing?" Prince said.

"One of these days being a little man ain't gonna save you," Fieldspar
said. Then he turned to Emory. "What you doing here?"

"Trying to get some sleep," Emory said.

"That's cool," Fieldspar said. "That's fine with me."

He rapped the club a couple of times against his open hand and wandered off.

"I'm gonna knock his damn head off," Prince said.

Arnold laughed.

"You come on down to Texas with me," he said. "We'll go to a bar and
find you a little shit kicker with no arms for you to fight. That'd be just
right for you."

"I could knock your teeth out," Prince said. "Every one of 'em."

"Aw, Mitch, I didn't mean nothing by it," Arnold said.

"Could I come to Texas with you?" Prince asked.

"No, you can't come down there," Arnold said. "Besides, some clerk at
personnel told me they're cutting orders on me tomorrow. Get my free
ride to the front gate. You'll be here another week at least."

"You don't want me to come," Prince said.

"Not right away," Arnold said. "I'll write you. Let you know."

"I could help you train horses," Prince said.

"Maybe," Arnold said.

Prince slid off the bunk and began looking through his suitcase. When he climbed back up on the bunk he had a K-bar fighting knife in his hand.

"He comes back and I'll cut his balls off," Prince said.

Arnold laughed.

"Fieldspar will slap you right through that wall," he said.

Emory thought of retreating to the orderly room. Maybe the sergeant would just let him sit there the rest of the night. But if he did that he might end up on KP. They liked to grab transient troops who wandered in. Emory had been in the army long enough to know to stay out of orderly rooms.

"You watch my stuff," Emory told the pair.

He went out of the barracks into into the cold night air. The barracks had flower beds bordered with bricks set on edge. Emory pulled up a brick and returned. He showed the brick, which felt cold and heavy in his hand, to Arnold and Prince.

"I'm going to sleep," Emory told them. "Anybody fucks with me and I'll kill 'em."

"Man, I believe you," Prince said.

Arnold nodded in agreement.

Emory lay down and nestled the brick in his right hand. He closed his eyes and went to sleep, the strident voice of Prince in his ears.

Emory dreamed of the outpost. He was on watch and there was movement below. He popped a flare. As the parachute carried it out over the rocks below, he saw an ape scurrying across them and into the trees.

Then he felt himself falling, the bunk bed overturning with a crash. The barracks were dark. Someone yelled out Arnold's name. A voice close to his ear cursed. The other men were shouting. He pushed himself away from the bunk, still holding the brick tightly in his hand.

The overhead lights came on and in that instant of illumination, as if caught by a strobe, he saw Prince astride Arnold. Prince had the heavy-bladed knife raised in his hand. Arnold lay stunned and offering no resistance, his arms lowered.

"Stop!" Emory screamed.

The knife, seeming to move in slow motion, came down into Arnold's chest. Prince stabbed once, then twice. The third time the knife got stuck in Arnold's chest. Prince cursed and tugged at it with both hands. A kind of bubbling sound was coming from Arnold.

Emory lurched forward, his feet tangled in the blanket. Then he was free and reaching out for Prince, who had put his foot on Arnold's chest to gain leverage. Suddenly the knife came free. Prince lunged at him with it. Emory brought the brick up into Prince's face, the little man falling backward without a sound.

Then Emory had the knife and was on Prince, who had risen to his knees. Someone caught Emory's arm. He turned and looked into the face of Fieldspar.

"Just stop," Fieldspar said. "You want to end up like us?"

Fieldspar took the knife out of Emory's hand.

"That little bastard is fucked up on speed," Fieldspar said. "Thinks he's ten feet tall."

They stood around over the still body of Arnold, waiting for the MPs to arrive. Emory heard Prince screaming from the latrine, his voice echoing off the tile.

Emory thought of Arnold camped beside the river, blue smoke from his mesquite fire rising through the branches of the oaks, and of Prince, dressed in a double-breasted suit and wearing dark glasses, driving a big car fast on a perfectly straight highway across a desert vista. He looked at the rest of the men, all dressed in civilian clothes, and thought how each had made a wrong turn, their dishonorable discharges placing a mark on them that never could be erased. And he realized he hadn't escaped the war. It wasn't just that he might have killed Prince if Fieldspar hadn't intervened. Somehow up on that Pleiku mountaintop he'd lost clarity.

It was growing light outside the barrack windows. Off in the distance he heard the sound of sirens. Whether it was the medics or the MPs was impossible to tell. But he wished they could all, Prince included, climb to the top of the big volcano and there on the summit, amid that clean white landscape, the dry snow squeaking under their boots, stand and be bathed in the light from the rising sun.